SEAN

THE SONS OF CROSBY BOOK 6

KATHI S. BARTON

World Castle Publishing, LLC
Pensacola, Florida
Copyright © Kathi S. Barton 2020
Paperback ISBN: 9781953271280
eBook ISBN: 9781953271297
First Edition World Castle Publishing, LLC, October 19, 2020
http://www.worldcastlepublishing.com

Licensing Notes

Cover: Karen Fuller
Editor: Maxine Bringenberg

Prologue

Sandy waited to talk with her attorney. He didn't cost anything, and her experience on that seemed to be a person got what they paid for. But he seemed to have his shit together, for which she was very glad.

Of course, he didn't know the whole truth about anything that she'd done. Especially when it came to her past and the life she'd had with her children. Sandy didn't think that Rachel would say anything different, not if it kept her from going to jail again.

"You told me that your sister forged your name to legal documents, correct?" Another lie she'd told him, but he believed her. "You'd think that someone that works for the government would know better than to do something like that. I mean, that's serious jail time for her."

Sandy felt a little guilt for that, but let it go. Again, Rachel would want her to be with her kids, wouldn't she? That's all she ever talked about was how they needed their mom out of prison. Not that she wanted to hang around them much either, but it was either Rachel claimed that she was a wonderful mom or Sandy would end up in jail forever. Third time, she knew, was not a charm.

"Did you go and talk to her about it?" He said that no one was home. "It's Wednesday, right? That's pizza night at the house. That's probably where they are."

"I don't think so. According to the landlord, Rachel had him pick up her mail for a week and to make sure that no one got into their place. She even said not to allow you in. What's she hiding from you?" Rachel had taken her kids on a trip? Sandy wondered if there would be gifts for her when they returned. Then she remembered that she'd turned her kids over to Rachel. "Do you know where she might have taken them? I mean, if she forged your name to those documents, then she isn't allowed to take someone else's children across state lines. Did you know that?"

"No, I didn't." She didn't either. But now that Sandy thought on it, it would be like her sister to take the kids someplace special, to probably break the news of what she'd done. "You think she would have told them about the paperwork? I mean, not that she forged my name, but that she believes what she did is right?"

"If she did forge your name to those papers, then she'd be in trouble more if she took them across the state lines. We can attach kidnapping to what she's doing." Nodding, Sandy wondered if her sister would ever forgive her for this and decided that she would. Rachel had a soft heart. A soft head too, but it was her heart that she was playing around with. "I'll have someone check the airports for a ticket in their name. Maybe she's only taking them to an amusement park or something. But what we have to work on now is this shoplifting charge against you."

"I was so depressed about not seeing my kids." The attorney nodded. Sandy supposed that it helped her, too, that the man was a new dad. "I knew as soon as I did it that it was wrong, but you have no idea how it feels when you're not able to get a hug when you can."

Hugs. Sandy hated hugs more than she did nasty noses and dirty diapers. Her kids were well past that now, of course, and had been for some time. That was why she'd moved in with Rachel and the kids again because she figured that she'd be able to handle all their shit now. But it had been one thing after another with them.

Always with their hands out for something they needed for school. They needed a coat or boots before winter. Finally, she told them to see Rachel for that shit, cutting out the middle man, so to speak. Not that she didn't have the money, Sandy thought. Rachel had all kinds of money.

Sandy had tried her best to figure out how to take cash from her sister's accounts, or even to get a check to write out to cash. But Rachel was very careful of that, never leaving anything out where she could find it. Sandy was sure that Rachel was well aware that she'd been looking.

Rachel had always been stingy with her money. It was always like she was saving for something big. So far as Sandy could see, she'd not spent any of her money on anything bigger than a car, and even that was older than dirt. It didn't even have air conditioning.

"Did you hear me?" Apparently, she'd been daydreaming

again and told the attorney that she was sorry, just thinking about her children. "I'm sorry, Mrs. Farley. We'll get them back for you. But, we just found out that Rachel has gone to Ohio. Do you know anyone there?"

"No, I don't think so. But her job, they send her all over the place when they need her." He asked her what she did for the FBI. "I don't really know, to be honest. I know that she's been doing her job since she was just out of college."

"Well, it won't get her anywhere for much longer. I have someone from this office going there now to see what is what. If you hear from her, not that I think you will, being in jail right now, you give her my name and tell her that I wish to speak to her." It was then that Sandy realized that she didn't know the man's name. Not even a hint of it. Then he laid his card in front of her. "That's my direct number. You have one of the officers call me no matter when you hear from your sister."

"Is it important for you to know that she's not really my sister? Rachel is my sister-in-law by my dead husband." He said that it was important. "I knew Rachel long before I met her brother. Jonathon and I were married for about a year when he was killed."

"I'll make a note of that."

Sandy nodded and was glad that he'd not asked her how Jonathon had been killed. She'd done it while stoned out of her mind one night. Sandy didn't even know what the argument had been about. That was when her children had been taken from her the first time. Rachel had gotten them just before they'd been put in the system because she'd been put in jail for his murder. Not that anyone believed that she would actually kill her own loving husband. Rachel had helped her out with that as well.

When she was taken back to her cell, Sandy laid down on her cot. It wasn't as bad as everyone made it out to be when in jail. She kind of loved it. Three meals a day that she didn't have to cook or clean up after. A nice cozy bed that had as many pillows and covers as she wanted. The best part was she didn't have her kids around whining about this or that. And no sister nagging at her to get a fucking job, either.

~*~

Sean got off the phone with Ben Shore and looked across his desk to Rachel. She'd not said much since they moved into his home. It had made him laugh when she asked for a key to the room she was in. While he could have broken down any door that she put between them, he had Conner, his butler, call someone to put the lock on her door. She didn't seem to be any happier about that than she was anything else.

"Do you want it easy or hard? I can do either one for you." She told him that she wanted him to never lie to her. "I would never do that. Besides, I can't anyway. However, I can be gentle about the information that I have if you'd like."

"How is that not lying?" He told her that he'd tell her the truth but be nice and ease her into things. "I'm not my niece and nephew. Just tell me what you've found out."

"Your sister is in jail for shoplifting. To play on the sympathy of the courts, she's telling them that you forged her name to the documents you filed. Also, that you took them out of the state without her permission." She asked him how that would have been gentler. "I might have started off saying that your sister is full of shit and that if she touches one of those kids or you, that she'll live to regret it."

"I don't think you fully understand the meaning of gentle." Sean laughed and saw her smile too. "What happens now? I mean, I'm sure that someone somewhere is going to want to speak to me about my side. If they do, what happens to Becky and Jon? I don't want anything else to happen to them."

"I don't either. I'm going to talk with my brother, Ryan. He's an attorney and has been one for a long time. Longer than any sitting judge has. He'll have answers. Between him and Misty, my sister-in-law, they'll have something that we can work with."

Rachel got up and started walking around his office. He didn't say anything to her, letting her roam around while she thought. They were having dinner with his entire family tomorrow night, and he was sure she wasn't too thrilled about that either.

"Those men that hurt Becky have you found them yet?" He nodded when she looked at him. "And they've been dealt with? Legally?"

"No. Not legally, no. But they won't hurt anyone ever again." She just nodded, and he let out a long breath. "You'll meet Emerald tomorrow night. She's sort of our go-to person in finding people. When she caught up with them, they were doing the same thing. But this time, they didn't get far enough to hurt the young girl. She was eight. Emerald made them suffer a bit before—"

"I want you to tell me things gently from now on. Or better yet, I'd rather you said to me, 'You don't want to know.' I will know then that I really fucking don't want to know." He said that he could do that for her. "I don't know what's going on here with you and I. I know that you're not going to hurt me. I have a friend that I spoke to when we got here. She told me that you were one of the nicest men that she knew. Your whole family was people that could be depended on when the shit hit the fan."

"That's very true." Rachel sat back down in the chair. "Do you have questions? Or too many to ask?"

"Both. You said that you were old and powerful—what does that mean exactly?"

Sean wanted to tell her that she didn't want to know but thought that perhaps she did need to know just what she had at her beck and call.

"I'm thousands of years old. My family was powerful before we were given the gifts from Killian. With what she gave us, we were more than likely the most powerful beings in the world, with the exception of the queen. But since then, we've merged with a great many other creatures. Emerald is the queen of dragons. Protector of them, too, with the help of my brother." Rachel asked him if there really were dragons. "There are. Unicorns, as well as a few other creatures that people think aren't real. I can introduce you to them when this is all done if you'd like."

"I don't know. What else is in our corner?" He told her. "So there are faeries and brownies that we can call on, as well as an army of wolves. You do know that this is a lot for me to take in, don't you?"

"I do. But you're doing just fine so far." She got up to pace again. "I wanted to make you aware of something that your friend might not have known if she's not a vampire. I can no longer drink from anyone else but you. Ever again. In an emergency, I can drink from my brothers, but no one else."

"No, she didn't mention that." Sean nodded but didn't say anything more, waiting for Rachel to ask whatever she wanted. "You're wealthy, she told me. Beyond any wealth that anyone has ever been able to calculate."

"That's partly true. You're very wealthy too, now that you're my mate. The children too are wealthy, and I will do whatever you wish regarding them." She asked him what he meant. "If you'd marry me, which is no big deal to think about now, then everything that I own will be put in your name. That's to keep people, mostly people that aren't aware of what we are, from becoming suspicious of us being around so long. Then after a while, it will come back to my name. But I will forever think that whatever I have is yours, and whatever is yours is yours. In several lifetimes, Rachel, you could not spend all the money we have so that we'd have nothing. There is always money to be had. Legally."

"I need to think about this." He told her that he had no doubt that she did. "Where do I go when I have questions? To you? I don't want to take up your time."

"You can come to me whenever you wish. Or to any member of my family. They'll answer everything and anything you wish. But, like me, you'll have to tell them how you want your information. Also, the women in this family are very strong, like you are. And they'll be almost too much. But I have no doubt at all that you can stand up to them."

When she left to see to the children, he leaned back in his chair. He was nervous as fuck around her, and he thought she might know it. Sean was as excited as he'd ever been about having anyone in his life. He just hoped that he didn't have to kill anyone around her to keep her safe.

Chapter 1

It didn't take a genius to know that Rachel was in over her head. Not only that, but she was having difficulty figuring out the paperwork she'd come here to read. It had been written in Bosnian, then German, and now English. She'd bet anything that Bosnian wasn't the first language either. Christ, where had they gotten this thing?

Getting up from the table she'd been using, she looked around the house as she stretched. This was by far the biggest private home she'd ever been in. Not that she made a habit of going to private homes, but this one was large. Going to find someone to speak to about the papers, she was stopped in the hallway by the butler. Rachel had no idea what his name was right now, but he seemed to understand.

"Connor, miss. Is there something I can help you with?" Rachel asked after the kids. The man's face lit up like a tree. "They're in the media room with Lord Sean. He had us pop some popcorn, and they're watching the pregame. I'm to understand there is a large college matchup tomorrow."

"Yes, I've heard that as well." She hid her smile. "Is there anyone else from the Crosby family that I can talk to about this work?"

"No. I think Lady Brandy is coming over later, but she's not involved in the work you're doing. Shall I get Lord Sean?"

"If he's the only one I can talk to." She didn't want to disturb him or the kids. Last night she'd had a long talk with them about their mother. Sandy was causing all kinds of trouble for her and them. But so far, she'd been told to keep doing what she was here for and that the Crosbys had it under control, whatever that meant to a kiss of vampires. Sean came toward her just as she was going to go back to the table to work. "I'm sorry to interrupt you guys."

"It's all right. They know the players better than I do. What can I help you with?" She handed him the copies she'd been working on. "I'm not an attorney, but Ryan said to call him if you ran into trouble."

"Yes, well, I know everyone is getting ready for tomorrow. This couldn't have come at a worse time, I don't think. I love Thanksgiving, but this needs to be done too." Sean nodded and handed her back the paperwork. "I don't think this is the original wording. It's close, but not enough for me to think it was written in Bosnian." He followed her into the dining room, where she'd been able to spread out what she needed. Sean asked her what language she thought it was. "Well, to be honest with you, it looks to me like someone took a translation book and wrote this to make it look like Bosnian."

"Okay. I understand that. So the language is there, but it doesn't have the sentence structure right. Can you tell what it says if that's what they did?" She said she could, but genders and other nuances would be incorrect. "Good to know. I'm going to ask Emerald to come over with Brook, Jefferson's wife. I don't think you've met either of them, but just brace yourself for their...how should I say this? They, like the other sisters, don't beat around the bush when they have something to say."

She was laughing as he sat down at the table. Before she could ask Sean when he was going to call the two women, they just showed up in the dining room. Sitting down hard, she stared as one of them started talking to Sean about the three turkeys being fixed up at her house.

"I don't think they're going to be enough." Sean didn't even look up from what he was doing as he told one of them that was only counting the three at her house. "I know that, dumbass. I still don't think six turkeys are going to be nearly enough. Did I tell you that the pack is peeling potatoes and cooking them?"

"I knew that. Emerald, Brook, this is Rachel Daniels. She's working on the translation of this paperwork for the Feds." Brook told her hi, and Emerald just looked at her. "Emerald, don't scare her, please. She's my mate, and I'd like her to hang around long enough for the rest of the family to get to know her."

"I don't think you scare easily, do you?" Rachel told her she didn't think she did. "By the way, you have a bit of ability now that I think you can use. I don't know that anyone else in the family has it, but you and I do. Hold onto the paper, and I'll show you."

"All right." Sean told Emerald to behave again. She told

him to fuck off. "What am I supposed to do now?"

"Ask it." Rachel glanced at Sean, then back at Emerald. "Ask it what it says. I'm sure you've seen those stupid television shows where the letters kind of move around, and there is it. Just ask the paper what you want to know about it."

Feeling stupid, she looked at the paper and then at Emerald. She hadn't any idea if the woman was making fun of her or was serious. Rachel was out of her element right now. When encouraged again to ask the paper, she did it.

"Are you the original translation of this work?" She watched as the letters moved around until it said, in Bosnian, that it was. "Why are you written as gibberish?"

It took it a long time to answer her this time. She was just about to toss it on the table again when the letters moved to form several lines of words. As she watched and read them, Rachel read out loud what it was telling her.

"The person forced me to write this just as he said it to me. I hope that once you figure this out, you'll know there is nothing here for you to read except from a person trying to see his name put into the newspapers." She looked at Emerald and asked her why it had been given to Mel. The letters moved again. "The forceful person is just a boy looking for attention."

"How many man-hours have been wasted on this, do you figure? The little fucker is going to hear from me." Emerald looked around when Rachel cleared her throat. There stood Becky and Jon. "Hey there, kids. I'm sure you've heard someone pissed off before."

"Yes, ma'am." Jon sat down at the table with his sister. "I was wondering something. You don't have to answer us or anything if you don't want to. But Becky and I were wondering if there was some way that we can talk to our...Sandy. We both want to tell her that we don't want her messing this up for us like she did everything else."

Sean cleared his throat as he began speaking. "I can tell her that for you, Jon. I have to be honest in telling you I don't think it'll do a lick of good. Your mother isn't out for anyone but herself." Jon nodded as if he already understood that. Sean continued as both children looked down at their laps. Rachel hurt for the two of them. "I'd like you to meet my other sisters. This is Emerald, the woman I was telling you about, and Brook. She's not my sister by marriage or blood, but we all love her just the same."

"Whatever he told you, it's a fucking lie." Emerald sat down beside the two of them, and Rachel held her breath. The woman didn't give a crap who she was speaking to; she didn't hold back. "I want to tell the two of you something. Something that I want you to take very seriously. This house is a safe place for you to be. Any of our homes, the Crosbys, is a safe home. You can say whatever you want. Ask for whatever you want, and you can pretty much do what you want. Within reason. The reason I'm telling you that now is that you can't be safe anywhere if we don't know where you are. Do you understand?"

"You mean if we were to just get up and go out into the yard or something, we could be snatched. I've been raped before. It's not at all fun." Emerald told Becky she was sorry for that. "It was my mom that caused those men to do those things to me. She didn't have the money for her dope, and she traded me off for the money."

Jon took Becky's hand when no one said anything. "It wasn't her fault. My sister wasn't the one that caused her to get raped."

Sean stood up and went to Jon. Rachel had never seen him so angry before. But when Sean spoke to Jon, his voice was as calm as the hands he put on his shoulders. He, too, didn't seem to hold back with what he said to him. Rachel was afraid they might see violence as a way of dealing with things.

"Of course, it wasn't her fault. The men that did that to your sister, can I tell you something about them? It can't go any further than this room, all right?" Becky nodded, then Jon did. Rachel already knew that Emerald had killed them. She watched the kids as Sean spoke to them. "They're both dead. If you're going to ask me if they suffered, then I'm going to tell you that they did. For as long as they could be hurting, they were. They'd taken another little girl and were about to hurt her as well. They'll never hurt anyone, not ever again."

Jon seemed to understand before Becky did that it had been Emerald. He watched her with narrow eyes as he seemed to be summing her up. Once he seemed to have come to a conclusion about her, he stood up. Putting out his hand, he looked her in the eye.

"I thank you for what you did, Miss Emerald. I do. I used to think I'd do it, go after them and hurt them too. But I'm just a little kid and would more than likely have gotten my butt handed to me in style." Emerald went down on her knees and looked him in the face. "She's my sister, and they hurt her badly."

"I know they did, Jon. And I also know you would have been hurt badly too if you'd done that. You will remember, the next time someone hurts you or your family, that there are enough beings here that can kick their fucking asses to the moon and back, correct?"

"I know that. Now. I don't want to go back to my mom." Emerald said they were working on that. "You work really hard on it, Miss Emerald. She's a mean, nasty, selfish person, and I think if she was to get us back, we'd be dead sooner than later. I've never felt so good as when sleeping here without being afraid. Even though you have a potty mouth, I really like you too. I think everybody here would come to help us if we needed it."

"You're right. Anyone, and if necessary, everyone would come to your and your sister's rescue." He nodded, then hugged her. "You have no idea how much a simple hug can make a person feel good. You and your sister are not going to be hurt again."

After Emerald and Brook left, they were called to lunch. She wasn't sure she could eat anything, not after the emotional morning she'd had, but as soon as they entered the kitchen, her mouth watered, and her belly growled. Becky made fun of her, and Sean laughed.

"What do we call you?" Sean asked Becky what she meant as he got them both the glasses of milk they asked for. "Well, you're going to be with my aunt, right? I know you're going to have sex and stuff, so what do we call you?"

He nearly dropped the glass when Becky said that. Looking at her, Rachel was shocked too, but she knew the only answer she could give them was the truthful one. But she wasn't sure what the answer was. Laughing, she told Sean this one was up to him.

"Well, yes, in answer to your statement. We are going to have sex. While I'm not sure what you mean by the *stuff*, I'm sure we'll do that too. However, I don't want you to tell me what your version of the sex stuff is." Becky just smiled at him. "What to call me? Let me see. For now, you can call me Sean, or even Uncle if you want. The paperwork for you being adopted, from what I just found out, has been filed. The verdict is still out on whether or not it's done legally. It wasn't, but not the version that your mother is telling people."

"She's telling people that Rachel signed my mother's name to the paperwork because she wanted us. I don't care how we end up as yours and Aunt Rachel's, but I'm not going to go back with my mother. Never ever." Sean said they were working on that as well. "Good. She sold me once. I don't doubt that she'll do it again."

They ate their lunch and talked about school. They were both homeschooling for now, and that was fine with her. Rachel hadn't helped them with their studies, as they were both doing a very good job. Now that they were caught up, it was easier for them. When Sandy had them, she wouldn't make sure of anything to do with school or anything else for that matter. The kids really would be better off with nearly anyone than they would be going back to their mother.

When lunch was over, the kids went back to the media room. She had been in there before and thought it was the perfect place to watch a good movie or a game. Sitting back at the table, she picked up her phone to call Jamie to tell him what they'd found out. Sean asked her to hold on a minute, as he had a question as well.

"All right. But I'm not having any sex and stuff with you right now." He laughed, and she did, as well. "I'm sorry if they embarrassed you. I had no idea they were going to say that."

"It's fine. Really it is. But what I wanted to tell you is that Ryan is building a case against your sister. He wanted you to know that you might not be aware of is that Sandy is saying things about you that aren't true. That you beat the kids." Rachel was too shocked to say anything. "Also that when you took her kids away from her, you're the reason she robbed the bank where she was caught. She was depressed, and that was why she did it."

Rachel started crying. Why, she wondered, would her sister say something like that? Worse yet, why would people believe her? When she thought of all the things she'd done for her sister over the years, it hurt her that she could be so cruel to her. Not to mention the children.

Sean held her hand in his much larger one after handing her some tissues. "There's more. Are you ready?"

She shook her head. Going into the kitchen, she searched around until she found what she was looking for. The big bag of chips was torn open, and she started feeding her face. Stress was going to kill her; she just knew it.

~*~

Sean watched Rachel as she ate. Her tears hurt him, but he knew if he said anything to her at all, she'd break down. When she paused in shoving great handfuls of the salty treat into her mouth, she looked at him and asked what else she should know.

"First, I want to tell you that I love you. I know you might not be ready for that, but it's the truth. The second thing you should also be aware of is that you're immortal. I think you knew that, but I'm just putting it out there, in the event you should get into some sort of place where you could be hurt." She thanked him for that. Putting the chips on the table, she told him she was sorry. "For what? Being crushed by your own flesh and blood? I'm glad you've been taking this so well."

"She's not." He asked her what she meant. "Sandy isn't my blood relative. She's my sister-in-law. My brother, Jonathon, was her husband. Neither of them was all that good at taking care of themselves. I believe to this day that she killed him on purpose. Even after she spent some time in jail—that's when I took the kids out of the system—she claims it was an accidental shooting. I'm boggled by the fact that anyone believes anything that spews from her mouth."

"I can have someone look into the death of your brother as well." Rachel nodded. "Are you ready for some more news?"

"I know everyone thinks you're the greatest thing since sliced bread, but I'm not that trusting—not that much just yet—as I'm sure you've figured out. You are nice, I'll give you that, but I'm so stressed out right now that I just want to lash out at you and have you hit me or something." He said he would never hit her. "I know that too, on some level. I just need something, anything, to go right for me so I can feel better about that one thing. You have no idea how hard it's been the last year. Sandy, she's the worst kind of person. But those kids, they're amazing. I was terrified I was going to wake up one morning and find she'd taken off with them again. I don't know what I would have done had she done that."

"May I ask you why that has you wanting to lash out at me?" She told him she wanted him to show that he was pissed off because she'd brought all this to him. "You didn't bring this to me, Rachel. I barged into your life. I'm the one that wanted to and still wants to help you out of this mess. Jamie, you know him—he's pissed off enough for the two of us. He seems to have it in his head that had he not involved you in any of this, Sandy wouldn't have started this campaign to ruin you."

"Sandy would have turned this all around, no matter where I was." She put the chips away as she continued. "When I first brought Becky and Jon to my home, you should have seen them. Jon was sick with some sort of infection that hadn't been taken care of. He'd been that way for a couple of weeks. Becky, of course, was so stressed that I made sure she had help. I never knew about the rape until the other day. I wish now that I'd known about it. I'm not sure what I would have done, but you can bet that Sandy wouldn't have been around them again."

"Ryan, as I told you, is working on a case against your

sister. Slander is the most important thing right now. I'm to understand you gave him the letter, as well as copies of the adoption paperwork." She said he'd asked, and she'd handed it over to him. "That was smart of you to have kept it. It'll go a long way in showing the courts that you didn't do what she's saying you did."

"I have to be honest when I tell you I haven't any idea why I kept it. Usually, I just toss things out after I've finished with them. But this was important, so I filed it. I hate clutter. Where is Sandy right now? Do you know?" He told her what he knew. "That's a good place for her. She told me once that she loved being in jail. There wasn't anything for her to do other than to lay around and be fed three times a day. I couldn't believe she'd say something like that. But I don't believe a lot of shit she's told me over the last year. It's also why I've kept my checkbook and money locked away. I was positive she was hunting for them."

"You would know that better than anyone." She nodded. "Are you ready for some more information?" Rachel asked if it was important right now. "Nope. But if you ever have a question, I've said this before, you can ask me. Any of us."

"I know that." She wiped off the table. "I should know better than to eat something like that. It always gives me heartburn." She put her hand over her chest and said she didn't get it this time.

"You won't. Not ever again. Little things like that, I'm sure they're big to you, but you won't get sick at all. You're going to also find that you're a good deal stronger than you were before I touched you." She asked him about broken bones. "They'll break, and it will be painful, but they will heal almost as fast as they broke. Same with the kids. They'll never get sick either. I can't fix what they did to Becky. I'm assuming you know she has nightmares. But I can get her to someone that can speak to her about her rape that will help her deal with it better."

"I knew she had nightmares." She cocked her head as if she were thinking. "It just occurred to me that she's not had any since we've been here. Perhaps she is feeling safe. While I didn't know she'd been raped, I did know she'd been hurt." Rachel looked at him. "I wish I had a way of bringing that to light when I'm taken to court. I'd love to hear how Sandy tries and gets herself out of that one."

"I'm sure we can figure out something. Ryan and Misty, they're very good. Together they're unstoppable." She sat down again. "I would also like to tell you that tomorrow night, each of my family members will touch you and the kids. As we're so old and strong, we can find people with just a touch. In the event that someone tries to take one of you, we'll be able to find you a good deal faster. And at some point, I'll show the three of you how to reach out to any of us when you need to. It'll save you from having to make a call if you need something."

He told her anything that she wanted to know every time she asked. Sean was able to ease her mind on things she'd read about as opposed to knowing if they were true or not. She'd done her research and had a lot to go on, but there were things that, as mates, she hadn't been able to talk about.

Sean stood up when the front doorbell rang. "I'd rather

you didn't show yourself just yet. I'd feel better if you were to go into the media room with the kids until I deal with this." She asked him if it could only be his family. "They would have come right in, or they would have told me they were coming over. Please?"

"Yes, of course. I don't want anything to happen to any of us."

She went to the room with the kids, and he went to the door. Telling Connor that he had it, the man said he'd be there if he needed back up. Sean appreciated that right now. Who the hell knew who was coming to see him today.

The man standing there looked familiar, but who he was Sean didn't know. After asking him if he could help him, the man started past him into the house. Sean only had to put out his hand to stop him before he looked in his direction.

"I asked you what you wanted, not if you wanted to come in. Who are you, and tell me a good reason I shouldn't hurt you for trespassing." He told him his name. "That doesn't ring a bell with me. Am I supposed to know you?"

He did know. This was the infamous brother of the new chief of police, Jefferson Quinn. Sean waited for Charles to answer him while he told Jefferson who was at his door. The first thing Jefferson told him after cursing was to not let him in the house.

"I'm searching for my brother, Jefferson. Where the fuck is he? I heard he was hanging around here." Charles tried to move past him again. "You're not all that friendly, are you? I just want to get in out of the cold. Can't you allow me to get warm by your fire?"

"No. I can't. Your brother isn't here. Why would you even think he would be?" Charles told him not asked him to tell him where his brother was. "I'll do you one better. I'll call the police, and you can ask them. Move along or go to jail. This is not a good day to be testing my patience, Mr. Quinn."

"See, that right there tells me you're not as friendly as the townspeople said you were. They said that any of them Crosbys would lay down their life for someone they knew. You must be one that doesn't have any niceness inside of you." Sean didn't answer him. However, he did feel someone coming up behind him. "Hello there, little lady. Why don't you have your daddy here let me come in and get warmed up? I'm down on my luck, you see."

"My daddy will kick your butt all over the place if you try anything with him. He's not only going to hurt you if you don't behave, but he might just get you into an early grave. Why don't you go and bother someone else?" He wanted to turn and give Becky a hug for her bravery, but he watched Charles. "Dad, do you want me to call the police? I would really like to do that for you."

"That's an excellent idea, my dear. But don't say anyone's name where this guy can hear you. He might well try and use that against us at some point." She told him she'd be careful, and he heard her pick up the phone in his office. "You can leave here, but it's doubtful to me that you'll get far."

"I'm telling you right now, if I don't get to talk to my brother, I'm going to be causing you and that kid of yours all kinds of—" Sean didn't move when the cruiser pulled into his drive. It did startle Charles, but he seemed to think it was funny rather than scary. "She must have some kind of pull to have them here this fast. And would you look at that, there's my brother too. Jefferson, I was just hunting for you. Have you been arrested or something?"

"No. I'm the police chief here. Come away from the house, Charles, and I'll not have to shoot you. If this man is going to press charges, then I'll just get to take you in." Sean said he'd threatened his daughter as well as him. "Well now, that's a whole lot of different story. Billy, go on up there and cuff Charles for me. I'll keep an eye on him, so he doesn't try and pull some of his shit on you."

Becky came to stand by him, but not so she could be seen from the outside. She watched the man being arrested through the curtained window by the door. Then she reached out and took Sean's hand. He held her tightly and then asked her if she was all right. Nodding, she told him what she'd been doing.

"I know that man." He asked her from where. "I think he's been to the house before. I don't know when or why, but Jon might know. But he used to come by, and he and my mom would go into her bedroom. Then she'd come out stoned. I think that's where I saw him before."

Reaching for Rachel, he asked her to bring Jon to him at the door. She came out of the room with the young man and stood next to Becky, out of sight, as Jon looked out the front window into the yard where Charles was being arrested.

"Yes, sir, I know him. He's one of my mother's druggy friends. I've not seen him in a while, about a month or so, but that's one of the men. Mom called him a drifter. Said he drifted from state to state to get into trouble." Sean asked him if it had been a house his mother lived in or their aunt's. "My aunt's. Mom told us that Aunt Rachel knew about him coming by. I never thought to ask her about it. By the time he was gone, I didn't really think of him again. But that's one of them. Whenever any of her friends came around, we made sure to stay hidden even if she called one of us to come to her."

"How many other men came by the house, Jon? I'm not mad at you but at Sandy. I'm really sorry she did that." Jon said they were well hidden — no one would have found them no matter what — but that eight of them had come by. "Thanks, son. I hate that you weren't even safe in my home, but I'm so happy that you were smart enough to find a place to hide."

Rachel was hurt. Not by the kids, but that she'd not been able to keep men like the one in the yard away from the children. Rather than finding out shit that went down in bits and pieces, he decided that the four of them needed to sit down together and figure this out. It might even be helpful in the long run if they did know. At least enough that they'd be on the lookout for others that might be coming around. He was just glad he'd been able to stop Charles from coming into his home. There was no telling what he might have done if he'd been able to cross the threshold.

Sean looked at Connor. "Are you armed?" He said he could be if Sean thought it was necessary. "I do. I want everyone that works here armed from now on if they can be. I want my family safe from intruders. All right?"

"Very good, sir. There is a large number of outside staff

that should also be armed. I'm also a member of the local pack, and I'll ask if more of them can be roaming around until this is settled." Sean thanked him. "No need for that, sir. I've come to love your family, as well. And my missus, she thinks having the two younger ones here will help her as well. Our youngest just left home a few weeks ago."

After the police left, he took his new family to the living room. He thought it was time, perhaps well past time, that they all got on the same page concerning Sandy Farley.

Chapter 2

Sandy stretched out on her bed. She's overslept this morning, so was ready anytime they got off their asses to bring her lunch. The coffee she'd been able to have someone bring her wasn't the best, but it hit the spot. Thinking about the upcoming trial, she wondered how quickly she could get out and back to what she loved doing. They frowned on her having drugs while in her cell. Sandy was a little bummed out about the news she'd gotten last night. It seemed that her dear sister-in-law wasn't playing the way she usually did when it came to her.

"Your sister has hired an attorney to represent her in this case we're making against her." Sandy wasn't sure why that should matter, but apparently her attorney — his name wasn't right there for her to think of again — thought it was a big deal. "From the things they've brought to my attention, I don't think this is going to be as easy as you and I talked about. Ms. Daniels also has an attorney team on her side that I would just as soon not have to go up against. Crosby/Crosby has a solid reputation of never losing a case. Their background work on a case is legendary. Are you sure everything you've told me is the absolute truth? I don't want to go in there with lies that they're going to be able to cut through in the first five minutes."

Then she noticed his name badge. Willie Marks? What a stupid name, she thought.

"I don't know what it would be that they have on me. I'm not a perfect mother, but I have been there for my kids." Willie showed her some of the highlights, he called them, that had been brought to his attention from the prosecuting attorneys. One of them was that she'd left her kids in the hospital after they were born. "That was a mistake. Who wouldn't be overwhelmed when they found out they had twins instead of just one baby to take care of? I got them back, didn't I? I made up for it by being the best mother I could be."

"Did you?" She asked him what that was supposed to mean. "According to Crosby/Crosby, you were arrested for murdering your husband. That if not for your sister-in-law coming to speak on your behalf, you would have ended up on the wrong end of a prison cell."

"Yes, she did come to my aid then. I think only to snatch my kids. However, I don't know where they got that I killed him. It was an accidental shooting. The gun went off, and he was killed by it." He asked her who was holding the gun. While she wanted to tell him Jonathan had been, she knew that would get her caught in yet another lie. So she changed the subject. "You said this was going to be soon. Do you think she'll bring my babies to see me when she gets into town? I do miss them."

If pressed, she couldn't tell anyone their birthdate. Nor could she, Sandy thought, tell them anything personal about them. She knew they were twins but was so doped up when they were born that Sandy didn't know who the older was. Not even the color of their hair or their eyes came to mind. It just wasn't anything she ever thought was necessary to learn. However, she did know that Rachel would not only remember those things but even what she had gotten them for Christmas last year. All Sandy had gotten was a robe and a pair of slippers.

"I'm worried that Rachel is going to turn them against me. Have them tell lies, so they don't have to come home with me." He asked her what she could say that would make her own children not want to live with her. "I don't know. But she's done it before. Like she did tell them I was a doper. That's not true."

"Mrs. Farley, you were stoned when you were brought here this time. Also, I've been meaning to ask you, why did you revert back to your maiden name after your husband was killed?" She asked him if it was important. "It could be. You were married to their father, then you changed your name as soon as you were in prison the second time. There will be questions about that, I'm sure."

"Oh. I guess I just thought, at the time, that my kids would be better off not knowing about me. I have since changed my mind, of course, but it's really expensive to have your name changed back." She didn't know if it was or not, but it sounded good. Also, she'd been married to Jonathon, but she never took his name on anything. Now that was going to bite her in the ass. "Also, since at that time they were with Rachel, I thought it might work out better for them. At least that's what Rachel told me when she told me about forging my name to the paperwork."

"You said you'd not known about that until I brought it up." She did? Sandy had to think. "Mrs. Farley, you must keep telling me the truth. I can't have you telling me one thing, then a few days later tell me something else. It's difficult enough trying to keep you from going to prison."

"They'll put me in prison? I thought you were working on this, so I'd not have to go." He said he was working on a lot of things, one of them getting her children back from Rachel. But she had admitted to shoplifting, and that was it. "So why do I need to get the kids back if I can't use them?"

"What did you just say?"

Sandy started sobbing instead of answering him. She had to remain calm, or she was going to blow this before she was able to get Rachel here to get her out of this cell. She did like staying in jail, but that was only on a short time thing. Prison was too long term for her.

"It's all right, Mrs. Farley. I know you're stressed out."

The two of them worked on her plea, as well as what she was going to say to the judge. Asking if her kids would be there, Willie told her he didn't know. This wasn't about the children, as they were minors. That would be up to the judge.

As soon as she saw her lunch tray coming toward her, Sandy washed up her hands. They'd not leave it for her if they didn't see her washing up. It was the stupidest rule she'd ever been made to follow. Who cared if her hands were dirty or not? She was the one that was going to be eating with them. As soon as she was able to pick up her tray, she noticed how light it felt to her. Pulling off the cover, she was disappointed to find she had another sandwich.

Sandy asked her what was up with not having extras when the woman handing out trays went back by her. Yesterday she'd had soup and a sandwich, as well as two drinks and three desserts. The woman told her that was her meal.

"I don't understand." The guard stopped pushing the cart that still had trays on it and looked at her. "Is there someone in charge that I can talk to? This isn't nearly enough to keep me going until dinner. I missed my breakfast too."

"Did you really have some perverts rape your daughter for drugs?" The question startled her so much that she nodded before she could think to deny it. "Yeah, we all thought that would be something you'd do. We have access to all your files here. Did you know that? And to the stuff that is sent here for your attorney to pick up when he sees you. You can bet that before he left here today, we handed that right over to him. Not only did it give the information about how you'd not taken her to the hospital, but that your son had to take her. And there was a signed avadavat from the doctor telling that he'd treated her for rape. She was only ten years old, you monster. You're just lucky we're feeding you at all."

Staggering away from the bars, she sat down on her cot. Fixing up her food so that she could eat it, Sandy tried to think how the hell she was going to explain that away. While she devoured her food, she had one or two ideas that would work, but only if she could see what else was said about her in the files. Christ, she thought, her own kids were getting her into trouble.

She'd take care of them, she thought, especially Jon, when she got out of here. He was a fucking bugger, always watching her when she had men over. Making him promise that he'd not tell Rachel had taken her beating him before he agreed, but he'd not opened his mouth. She'd bet that right now, he was singing out everything she'd ever done while Rachel was working. Fucker.

After eating her lunch, which wasn't nearly enough, Sandy worked out in her head how she was going to explain the rape. It was not like Becky was hurt all that badly by the men. Christ, the way she hollered she made it sound like they were killing her. Neither of them had all that big of dicks. Becky was just lucky that her good buddy Charles hadn't been the one she owed money to. Now that man had a dick that made a woman wet just thinking about it.

"It was to help her mom, right?" That shouldn't be a reason she'd be in trouble. Of course, no one thought along the same lines she did. Prudes, she thought. Every fucking one of them.

By the time lights were turned off in the hallway, she thought she had it worked out. It was wrong, she knew, but Sandy was going to tell them that Rachel had been gone, and the landlord had wanted an advance on the rent. Not sure how that would work, she still thought it would. Since she didn't have the extra money, she'd sold off Becky. Yes, she loved that idea.

It had occurred to her that someone might ask the landlord,

but she didn't think they'd care enough to do that. She was on easy street for that anyway. Who the hell even knew who the landlord was? Not her. She'd bet Rachel didn't either.

Her sister-in-law was going to have to forgive her for a lot of shit when this was over. But Rachel would really want her to be with her children. That's why she had her living with them in the first place. She'd love it and hate it too, but it would be better for them. Sandy would have her kids, and they'd be helping their mother get some shit together. Not her life, but everything she wanted.

Closing her eyes, she thought of getting out of there. With her record, she'd have to be very careful not to get caught again. She might be able to pull the wool over the eyes of a lot of people, but not if she kept getting caught.

Perhaps she needed to just move to another state, a place where she'd be happy and could start over. Someplace warm that had a beach. Sandy thought about taking her kids with her — they'd be good for a buck or two. But really, they were a lot of trouble. Like from the day they were born, they had caused her nothing but grief — her sister-in-law too. How she wished she'd been out of jail when she realized she was pregnant.

It was too late for even a late term abortion by then. Even after she was let out, she was hog-tied to a woman that made sure she wasn't harming the kids. Then, when she'd found out about having two of them rather than just one, she freaked the fuck out and left the hospital. That was the dumbest thing she could have done. It was too late after that to see if she could have sold them off.

Sandy didn't think of things like that until it was too late. That had been the story of her entire life. Even marrying Jonathon had been a mistake. He was stupider than she'd imagined, and he didn't have shit to his name. It had been Rachel that had all the money, as well as the house he'd stayed in. Fucker had lied to her. But she sure fixed him, Sandy thought with a smile.

~*~

Dinner was much better than he thought it would be. Sean wasn't sure if it had anything to do with having his own family there or not, but it did help. The game on television was turned up loud, and the shouts around the room were even louder. Becky was right in the thick of things with his brothers and himself. Emerald was scary when her team didn't do as well as she wanted them to do.

They all laughed when Chase spoke to his wife. "Honey, I know you want to go there and tell them how you want them to play, but please don't. They're only college kids." Everyone laughed with him. "Promise me you'll keep your opinions here and not direct them to the coach."

"They need to win faster." She glared at Chase, and he couldn't help it; he laughed. "I could send you there to show them how's it done. Would that make you laugh it up, jerkoff?"

"Honey, it's been way too long since I've played football. Even the helmets are different from when I played." Sean told her she could take her frustrations out on the punching bag that had been hung outside just for her. When her face pinked up, he knew she'd already broken it. "You did it, didn't you?

You busted your bag."

"It was a particularly terrible day, and I didn't hold back." She smiled at him. "Chase has one filled with concrete now. It works much better for me."

Only Emerald would think that taking your frustrations out on a concrete filled punching bag would be better for her.

Before the game hit halftime, they were all called to dinner. He was thrilled about it. The scents coming from the kitchen and dining room were making him feel hungrier than he thought he really was. Jon came to have him help him with his plate, and Becky went to her aunt. He felt bad when Jon told him he didn't know what most of the food on the table was.

"All right. Why don't you take a little bit of whatever you think looks good and then do a taste test?" He asked if anyone would be mad if he didn't like something. "Nope. Not even when it's not Thanksgiving. But you can't just form an opinion on how it looks. There are things that might not be pretty to eat but taste amazing."

Jon nodded and did just what Sean said, taking little bits of food. Sean told the young man what it was he was eating. Helping him to the table, Sean made sure he had what he wanted to drink. The kids, both Jon and Becky, seemed to love milk.

Leaving Jon to his meal, he filled up two glasses of tea for him and Rachel. He noticed that Becky was having a hard time picking what she wanted, so Sean suggested doing what he'd told her brother. Rachel seemed as excited about that as the kids did. He, however, knew just what he wanted, and put a slice of bread in the middle of his plate and piled mashed potatoes, gravy, as well as turkey into a mountain of food. He'd go back for veggies at round two.

"That looks amazing. Is it good?" Sean cut her a bite and fed it to Rachel. "Oh, Sean. That is wonderful. I'm going to get that the next time. The macaroni and cheese is my favorite so far."

The two of them shared their food. Rachel was having so much fun that he got up when Jon and Becky needed refills on their milk or more food. Jon loved just about everything, with the exception of the cranberry sauce. Becky didn't care for turkey, but she loved the ham. Their seconds consisted of the things that they liked this time. And they were also sharing things off each other's plates.

The other kids seemed to be enjoying their new cousins. He was happy when they seemed to be laughing and having as much fun as the adults were. Sean wanted to pull them from the table and hug them all, but he also knew he'd embarrass them.

After the food was covered and put away for grazing, he helped his brothers load the dishwasher. There would be more plates and such later and throughout the day, but for now, they were cleaning the bulk of it up.

He was just putting the last of the pots away when his brothers turned to him.

"What?" Ryan asked if he could talk business with him for a moment. "If you think it's necessary, then yes. However, if Dad hears you, he's going to kick your ass."

They all laughed. When Ryan asked him to have a seat,

he had a feeling that whatever he told him, it wasn't going to be good news. When the rest of them had a seat, he braced himself for the news.

"We've had the body of Jonathan exhumed. Sandy is telling anyone that will listen that her husband was holding the gun when he was shot. No one did any kind of autopsy to make sure of that, but Misty thought it might be a good idea to do it because of everything else that is going on. It looks like he was murdered. Also, he didn't have any drugs in his system from what we've figured out, so her claim that he did it while stoned isn't going to stand up in court. The gun residue that should still be there isn't on his hands. The coroner had wrapped his hands up and left them that way when he was entombed. We think he might well have had the same idea we did, that she killed him." He knew why it was important but asked his brother. "It shows she has been lying about that from the beginning, and her word on anything isn't trustworthy. I've also spoken to her attorney, Marks. He called to tell me that he got all the information we had sent him and asked if he could put a deal on the table for her. He doesn't think she's going to take it, but he wanted to know what we could live with."

"I take it you want me to talk to Rachel about it." Ryan said that was what Misty was doing now. "I see. I don't really, but why is it you thought I needed to know like this? I mean, if you're telling her already."

"We wanted…. I wanted you to be prepared in the event she asks you about it. I know you never really liked being an attorney all those decades ago, but you do know what Sandy getting a deal could mean. Shorter prison terms. She could also demand to see her children. I would count on that if she's fighting this hard to get to see them." Sean said he'd not count on that. "Why not? You know something I don't?"

"Yes. The fact of the matter is, she doesn't want the kids. Rachel and I spoke about this last night, and she thinks her sister's plan is to take them and sell them. Rachel is afraid that is her plan, and the reason she's now claiming that, rather than Sandy forging the paperwork, Rachel did it." Ryan leaned back in his chair, and Chase got up to pace. They were all thinking that now, he'd bet. "I'm not positive she won't agree to the deal, but I'm reasonably sure Rachel wants her sister-in-law right where she is. Did you know she was not aware of Becky being raped?"

"I only just found out." The rest of them hadn't known either. Jason asked him if he was serious. "Yes. Apparently, Sandy was way behind in paying her dope dealer and told him if he'd wipe it clean, he could have Becky. They had to tie Jon up to keep him from tearing the man apart. That's why he's so protective of his sister. He's worried about her. I've been looking into getting her some help, someone that can deal with this sort of trauma. If you guys know of anyone, let me know."

The rest of the kitchen clean up was done in quiet speculation. They'd ask him or Ryan a question, but for the most part, everyone was thinking. Before they left the kitchen, however, he told them all not to say anything or treat Becky any differently. She'd know that they knew.

"I want to take them both in my arms and hold them

forever." He told Grayson he did as well. "What sort of monster does that to their own child, Sean? And figures it would be all right with them later in life? Christ. Humans are so cavalier about life. I wonder if anyone thinks about how their actions today will affect their family in the future."

When they left the kitchen, the football game was in its last quarter. When Becky and Jon, with the rest of the kids, joined them to watch, Sean had to poke a couple of his brothers to make them pay attention to the game. They were staring at his kids like they were afraid they'd break down or something. Finally, after about ten more minutes of him drawing them into the things going on around them, they started acting the same as before.

I have a question for you. Sean smiled when Rachel reached out to him. *You know, I do have to admit, this is much nicer than running around trying to find you when I have a question. Did you know the pack has a progressive teaching program? And that Becky and Jon have been invited to be a part of it?*

I knew about the program, but not that our kids were going to be a part of it. They want to, don't they? She assured him they did. They liked the kids there better. *Good. They'll be well protected there. With all those shifters around, they'll learn a great deal about all sorts of nonhumans as well.*

Maybe I need to join too. She was quiet for several seconds, and he waited. The game they were watching was a blowout for their team, so it was sort of boring. *Misty asked me if I'd like to offer a deal to Sandy in exchange for prison time. I don't know that I want that any more than I want her around the kids. But I'd hate for them to find out about it and hate me for keeping their mom in prison. Do you think I should talk to them about it?*

I do. But I think you're wrong about how they'll feel about it. I think they've had enough of their mother about as much as you have. She said she was sad about that. *But it's nothing she didn't bring on herself. You have to keep telling yourself that. The fact that she has been able to keep her kids for as long as she has is surprising to me.*

Do you think she'll win with this? I mean, I want her put away — that's why I think she'll be able to get out of this. He said he thought Sandy would be lucky if she didn't get several lifetimes out of this. *Did Ryan tell you they exhumed my brother? I guess she killed him as well. There wasn't even any gun residue on his hands. All the things I did for her.... All the things she told me, Sean, were lies. Everything, including how my brother was killed.*

Sean could feel her pain and got up to find her. Emerald and the other women were in the dining room having tea, and they told him she was out on the deck. Going out there, he found her just on the edge of the deck, talking to Killian. The two of them seemed to have become close friends. They both turned to look at him when he opened the door.

"I'm sorry. I was just looking to make sure Rachel was all right." Killian asked him to have a seat too. "I don't want to intrude."

"Come on. You're not. I was just telling your lovely mate here about the things you and your family do for us. Fairaday is coming to see her too. You've been remiss, young Sean, in showing your mate off to those around you." It wasn't a scolding, but he told her he was sorry. "That's fine. It's going to give me a chance to show her off. Spud, he's gone to

Fairaday for us."

"Killian told me if I ever needed a few minutes alone, she'd take the children to her side of the world. I was just telling her how jealous I'd be if they got to see unicorns before I did." He could hear the disbelief in her voice and was glad to see Fairaday coming through their yard on that very thing. "Sean! They're real! Look, it's a flipping unicorn!"

After petting the unicorn for a few minutes, she had him go in and get the children. No one was more impressed with the dainty little horse than Jon was. Not only did he have a long conversation with Fairaday about her job, but she allowed him to call her if he ever needed someone to talk to. Becky, Sean noticed, was talking to one of the many other faeries that had come along to see what all the excitement was about.

"Sean, Maybell said that she could be my faerie if I wanted her to be." Sean could bet he could power the house with the excitement in Becky's voice. "She told me she'd make sure I was protected and that I knew the rules of other creatures. I told her how Jon and I wanted to be veterinarians together. She said they were forever looking for someone to be a doctor for the other creatures."

He knew that, as a doctor, one of his sisters could take care of the animals should they be hurt. Sean had an idea that no matter what his two children decided they wanted to be when they grew up, they'd give it their all. They would have learned that from their aunt. Getting down to her level, Sean asked her if she knew the responsibility of knowing so much about other creatures.

"Yes. I'm to tell no one what I know. Not even if they

dig out my fingernails with a pair of plyers." Rachel asked her where she'd gotten that thought from, and Becky looked at him, wide-eyed. "I forgot we weren't supposed to tell her that we watch horror movies with you. She's not mad at you, Sean. I'll talk to her about it later."

"You do that." His thinking was that if the children saw some horror movies and how others like him were treated in them, they'd be more tolerant. They did point out how stupid the movies were too. "I'll talk to her too. I'll tell her that you and your brother are braver than I am when we watch them."

Winking at her, it was funny how things were settled up. Not only did Maybell become Becky's faerie, but Jon asked if he could have someone like Spud. No one understood that until Spud admitted that Jon wanted an older faerie, someone he could talk history with. Sean wondered if Jon realized that all the creatures there today were hundreds of years older than he was.

Chapter 3

Charles wondered if he was being picked on because of his brother, or if the cops around here treated every newcomer this way. Each time he asked a question, he was told he had to read the rules hanging over his sink. Sure they were. He'd seen them. What he wanted them to tell him was if he got special treatment or not. Charles was perplexed as to why, even though his brother worked in the jail, he'd not seen hide nor hair of him

"I should get something special, being how my brother is the chief of police." The woman down from him on the other side screamed that if he got extra food, she wanted it as well. Something about the old broad made him think he should know her, but he couldn't recall where he'd met her. "Shut up, you old fart. I'm not getting anything extra, so you're not either."

They'd brought her in a few days ago, he'd been told, so she could get a fair trial. Also, something about her having family here. It was doubtful there was anyone in the world unaware of her. She never shut the hell up. Another slight memory touched his head, but he couldn't catch why he should know Loud Mouth.

"Blow it out your ass, you jackass."

They'd been arguing since he'd gone by her cell, and she told him to grab the gun from one of the officers and give it to her. He couldn't figure out how that was supposed to work, what with the cops right there hearing every word she said. Ignoring her hadn't been easy either. Every time one of the cops came down their hall, she'd start yelling about her kids. He wondered if she realized that kids didn't want to see their parents in jail.

Hearing her yelling at someone coming through the door was like having a doorbell on the sucker. She'd scream, literally scream at them, then beg for more food. Charles had to wonder if she was a huge woman the way she always wanted food. When the cop stopped in front of his cell and opened the door, he sat on the side of the bed.

"You're free to go, Mr. Quinn." He didn't move, fearful that this was going to be a trap or something. "You are to stay one hundred yards from the Crosby family. If you're not sure if someone you see is a Crosby, you're to stay away from that person as well."

"Am I allowed to see my brother before I leave? He owes me some money." The cop told him he wasn't there. He'd planned it that way. "I guess that means he didn't leave me any money either. How does he expect me to get around if I don't have anything to use to get me some food and a place to stay?"

"I'm thinking he might just want you to find your own

way. That's what I'd do if my brother just got out of prison and ended up in my jail." He didn't care for the man's tone and told him that. "Really? I hurt your little feelings? I'm so not sorry. Get up and get out of here, Mr. Quinn, before I get you for trespassing."

"You're real brave when you're an armed man, aren't you? Why don't you meet me outside, and we'll settle this like men?" The cop told him he wasn't a child in a schoolyard anymore. He reminded him too that he was not to rob the banks in town or anyone else. "You sure do have a lot of rules around here."

"Actually, those are all things you should be following anyway. Believe it or not, people, nice people, don't have to be reminded not to rob places." The door was opened wider, and Charles got up to leave. Lunging at the cop only made him laugh. "You really are a moron, aren't you? Why on earth would you think I'd be afraid of you? A mere human?"

"You aren't human?" The cop let just enough of himself go so that he could see that he was a wolf. "What the hell is this world coming to when normal people have to hang around with nonhumans?"

"I have no idea. I've been asking that same question since I started working here."

Charles was out the front door with what little belongings he had come in with when he realized the guy had misheard him. Shaking his head, he walked to the store just across the street from the jail.

He wanted some fruit in the worse kind of way. An apple. Ever since he'd been a little tyke, he'd feel the cold air around him and want an apple. Most of the time, he'd not care for fruit—just an apple in the fall.

As soon as he entered the store, the man at the register came around to his side of the counter and asked him what he wanted.

"I'm just browsing." He didn't have money to buy anything with, but he wasn't going to tell this jerk that. As he walked around the store, trying to get a bead on where the apples were, the man followed him step for step. Finally, Charles had enough. "What the hell are you doing? Don't you have other customers you can bother?"

"I'm keeping an eye on you. We were all told this morning that you were broke and that you might come in and try to steal from us. I'm making sure you don't get anything from me." Charles asked him who would have told him that. "The chief of police. He's a great man, Jefferson is. You should have strived to be more like him."

Charles wanted to just swipe his hand over the pretty display of Christmas stuff. He mumbled about it not even being Thanksgiving when the man told him it was just yesterday. He'd missed the holiday? His favorite one? Not getting invited to his brother's house wasn't anything that surprised him, but he hadn't even gotten something special in his cell from the cops. What the hell was this world coming to?

Getting the same treatment all over town, he decided he might have to have a little talk with Jefferson. The nerve of him making sure everyone in town knew just who he was. What really pissed him off was the poster he'd seen in one of the shops he'd been in. It had a picture of him with his prison uniform on when he'd been put there, as well as his name. Under that, it said, "No money. No credit cards. No job."

The issue he had was that not only did he not have a clue where Jefferson lived, but he didn't know what car he drove when he was off duty. Deciding he'd go over to the jail and wait for him to come to work, he found himself a seat outside the library and sat down. It was cold—fucking cold, as a matter of fact—but he needed his brother so he could explain a few things to him. Like to stay the fuck out of his life.

There seemed to be a lot of activity going on around town today. Of course, he had no idea if this was normal or not, but a lot of people were going in and out of shops and seemed to be in good cheer. Charles hated Christmas. He liked it when he got something, but when people put out their hands wanting something in return, Charles wanted to knock their heads off.

He saw the little girl he'd seen at the house that had called the cops on him and started to go to her. Charles didn't know what he had planned to say to her, or for that matter, what he might have done to her. But he stopped standing up while his body was still bent and looked at her.

She stared at him like she knew just what he was thinking. His balls tightened up to his body when she did that eye thing at him, telling him she had her eyes on him. But he had a feeling she wasn't just giving the sign—she was actually going to be keeping her eyes on him. Charles sat back down when she turned and walked away.

Having his heart pound like he'd been running a race

didn't help him at all with his feelings. No matter how many times he told himself he wasn't afraid of her, Charles knew he was on some level. Looking around to make sure she wasn't sneaking up on him, he cried out when he saw a woman standing right behind the bench he was on.

"You scared the shit out of me. What the hell are you doing sneaking around like you are?" Instead of answering him, she sat down on the seat next to him. "I don't remember inviting you to have a seat. I'm waiting for someone. Unless, of course, you're here to service me? I could use a good blow —"

The smack to the back of his head was a lot more painful than he thought it should have been. Looking at her again, he asked her what the hell was wrong with her. She smiled, and he felt the same fear he had with the little girl. Ball tightening fear that made his dick hurt.

"I'm going to tell you a few things. A few things that you should take to heart, so you live just a little longer." She looked at him, then at the store where he'd seen the girl go in. "That little girl is my niece. Stay away from her. I'm not going to threaten you in any way, but I make you a promise that if any harm at all comes to her, you will suffer in ways you cannot imagine."

"You bad enough to make that happen?" All she did was smile and then nod at something across the street. The man standing there was the same ass that hadn't allowed him to come into his house. "So? He's a pussy, like the rest of the men around here."

While he watched, the man was suddenly in front of him. Not even a sheet of paper could have come between them; he was that fucking close. Trying to back off a little, Charles was just afraid enough to make sure he didn't touch him. When he disappeared, Charles looked at the woman again.

"You'll be careful now on touching anyone I love. That would include that man's brothers. They'll kill you in ways so your own mother wouldn't be able to identify you when they're finished." Charles asked her why she thought he should be warned. "Because I know who you are. Who you're connected to as well. Does the name Sandy Farley ring a bell?"

It hit him then. "The woman in the jail with me. Christ, she's gotten huge. What the hell has she been eating? Other people?" He laughed, but the woman didn't join him. "Oh, come on now. You have to know that's funny. She used to be this skinny bitch that was high as a kite all the time. Now you'd think—well, she's gotten fat."

"That girl over there is her daughter." He tried to remember if he'd ever seen her at the house. When nothing came to him, he asked why he'd care. "Because when Sandy goes to prison for all the shit she's done, you're going with her. Unless, of course, you play ball with me."

"What's in it for me?" She told him he got to be free for a little bit longer. "Being free without any dough isn't really all that fun. What kind of money are you offering me if I help you with convicting her?"

She stood up, and he waited. When she simply walked away, Charles called her back. But she didn't turn in his direction, nor did she say another word to him. It wasn't until he saw a cruiser going by him that he thought perhaps she'd been right in one thing. If he decided not to help her, he was going to have the police up his ass the entire time he was in this town.

Charles had no idea how he could help her without getting himself in deeper shit. He'd not only supplied Sandy with enough drugs to kill a horse most times, but he also helped her out when she needed a partner in crime. The last thing he remembered doing with her was robbing the convenience store not far from where she'd lived. That had to have been a few years ago.

He had seen her a couple of times off and on before he'd fucked up and ended up in prison this last time. They'd fuck like donkeys, the two of them, and then he'd give her drugs. If there were kids in the house back then, he'd not heard a sound from them. It's not like they wouldn't have heard the two of them. Sandy was a screamer in all things, he supposed.

Finding himself a place to stay was going to be near impossible. There were places he could flop, but nothing that had heat and running water. It wasn't like he was fixing to take a shower or some shit like that, but he did, on occasion, need to clean himself up.

Thinking about his situation, he realized he'd more than likely missed Jefferson going into the station house. Jefferson had always been a goody-two-shoes person. Not even when they were kids had he wanted to have any fun. He thought about the one and only time he'd tricked Jefferson into helping him rob the next door neighbor. Not only did Jefferson tell on him, but he even worked to pay for the things Charles had broken in his attempt to get out of the house ahead of the man with the shotgun.

"Fucker."

Walking around, Charles could see several buildings that were being worked on, but nothing he could use for a few nights to have himself a warm place to stay. Not only did the signs outside of the construction sites proclaim that there were cameras all around, but dogs were roaming the premises when they were done for the day. Charles thought everyone and their brother had cameras out now. It was getting so that a dishonest person couldn't tamper with mail anymore too.

Just as he was going to see about sneaking into one of the older buildings that at the moment wasn't being worked on, he saw Jefferson. He was with a pretty little woman, and they were holding hands. Charles wondered what that was all about until he saw the woman kiss Jefferson before she went into the drugstore just down from the station.

"Hey, Jefferson? I gotta talk to you." He crossed the street, unmindful of the traffic, and nearly got himself T-boned. Cursing at the guy, he nearly lost Jefferson when he started walking back to the station house. Catching up to him, Charles told him to hang on a minute. "I need someplace to stay and some money. Now, Jefferson. I'm hungry and cold, and you're going to give me some relief."

"No." Jefferson turned on his heel and walked away. Catching up with him again, Charles grabbed him by the shoulder to turn him around. Jefferson looked at his hand, then at him. "Remove your hand from my person, Charles, or I'll remove your arm and beat you to death with it."

"Christ, is everyone in a shitty mood nowadays?" Jefferson told him it might just be him. "Nah. People love me.

Hand it over. I don't have the time or the energy to fuck with you right now. Why did you wait until right before lunch was served before you let me go? I got nothing here, and you're going to help me out."

"I'm not going to do shit for you, Charles. I don't know if you remember this or not, but you're a grown man and should be looking out for yourself." He asked him about the broad he was with. "My wife."

Nothing else. Not when he'd been married or what her name was. It was like the rest of the town—they didn't want him to know shit. Charles told Jefferson that he'd put him up for a few days and make sure the little woman fed him. Instead of telling him his address, Jefferson just walked away.

"I'm getting sick of people pretending like I'm not talking, Jefferson. You might want to remember this warning I'm giving you. I surely would hate for something to happen to that new little family of yours." Instead of turning back and telling him to back off or something along those lines, Jefferson laughed, like it was the funniest thing he'd ever heard. "This shit is getting old. I'm going to have to teach someone a few lessons."

He didn't know how he was going to do that, or for that matter, who he was going to mess up. But someone was going to have to take him seriously, or they'd be deader than a doornail. Whatever the hell that meant.

~*~

Sean was hunched over his desk when he realized someone had come into the room with him. Turning to see who it was, he saw that Jon had come in. How long he'd been there, Sean didn't know, but he'd made himself at home, apparently. Clearing his throat caused Jon to look at him and smile.

"You really get into your work, don't you?" He said he did, but this was something special. "Yeah, I got that. Did you know you talk to yourself? I know Aunt Rachel will love it, whatever it is. I know you're worried about that on account of you asking yourself that over and over. I have a problem I need to talk to you about."

"All right. Is this problem going to entail me killing someone for you?" Jon laughed and said it wasn't really a problem, but a dilemma. "To keep me from guessing a bunch of stuff that's wrong, why don't you tell me about it?"

"I know that you and your family are planning a huge Christmas. Misty was measuring me for clothes and stuff. You really think she'll get me clothes? Anyhow, I was wondering how a kid like me would be able to make some money to be able to buy a few presents. Not a whole lot of people, but a few. Is it all right that I call your dad Grandpa? He wants me to, I can tell." Sean asked him which of those were the dilemma. "Oh yeah. The money. Clothes will be all right, I guess. I surely don't need any, not with you and Aunt Rachel getting us so many, but I'll love them. Also, the grandpa thing. That's not a big deal unless you're going to say no, then I'll have to tell you that it's already going on. Becky and I, we decided he's the only grandpa we're going to get, so we're going to call him that."

"Good to know. I doubt that Dad would care if I had an opinion about what you call him anyway. He's been begging to be a grandda since Jason got married." Leaning his back against the table, he asked Jon what sort of job he was looking for. "I know you will have to do your homework before the job. And if your grades slip, then the job will have to be put off until you bring them back up. That was something I heard on television a few days back."

"You sounded like a dad would, I think. Is that what you were going for?" Sean said it was. "Well, you passed as far as I'm concerned. One that pays good. I'm sort of getting a late start on making some cash. When we moved here, I thought it was going to be just for a little while, until we were safe. Now that it's full time, and I'm happy for that, I need to figure out something to catch up with gifts."

"What can you do?" Jon told him his only talent so far was making his bed and taking the trash out. "Those are admirable jobs too. Also, you don't want to forget that you take a shower nightly in addition to making your bed. Another thing that shouldn't be overlooked when you live with people that can smell you a mile away."

"Good point. I can sweep the floor too, but then I get dirty looks from the staff." He laughed. "Not really, but Becky said I need to stop looking for housework to do because the people that work for you are excited to be doing it for us. Is that right?"

"It is. Living with me all these years, they've not had an occasion to have to clean up after me. Cooking either." He said he got the cooking part. "So you can do pretty much anything domestic. Also, I noticed you help your sister with her homework. I'm very proud of you for helping her."

"It's a tradeoff. I help her with her social studies, and she helps me with math. I'm okay with math, but sometimes I need her to tweak me a little. That's what she calls it." Jon smiled at him. "Becky sure is happy being here. I am too, but I don't think she's been happy for a long time. She's also not having any nightmares. Maybell told me that she helps her when she starts having one. I think that's the best reason in the world for having a faerie around."

Sean was getting used to having a conversation with the kids. They could bounce off several subjects quicker than his dad could. And they'd be able to keep straight if you'd answered them or not. Jon was the most brilliant scatterbrained kid he'd ever met. Sometimes he'd listen to him talk to his sister just to be in awe of how they were so connected with each other.

"Jobs? There are a few things you can do for me in here. Remembering to take the trash out on trash days gets me into trouble when it starts piling up. I know it's not much, but it's a start. Who else have you asked about working?" He remembered that Killian had asked him for some help too. "Also, I know you've met the queen. She told me just yesterday that she could use some help with feeding the baby animals that were born. I don't know what that entails, really, but she did mention it."

"How do I get in touch with her? I don't mind taking your trash out on Tuesday nights." He laughed when Sean asked him if that was trash night. "It is. I saw that you had a lot on Monday, so I took it out with the rest of the stuff in the house. Why do girls keep the bags of stuff they get things in? I don't understand girls at all."

"I don't either. To get in touch with Killian, you only need to ask your faerie to make an appointment with her. Or you can go out into the lawn and dig your fingers into the dirt, and she'll answer you if she's not too busy." He tried to remember if he'd answered everything, and Jon asked him about the bags. "I don't know. Bags are bags, aren't they?"

"I don't know myself. The other day Becky nearly took my head off when I suggested that she throw some of them away. She told me they were treasured." Jon rolled his eyes. A typical reaction that most men had for women, Sean thought. "Anyway, I'm going to contact her in the dirt. Thanks."

After he left, Sean sat there for several minutes, thinking about having kids around all the time. They weren't so bad, he thought. Chase was bonkers about his kids, telling anyone that would listen that his two were sleeping through the night. When Sean told him that his two were as well, he got offended. Turning back to his work, he looked up when Jon came back into the studio with Killian.

"I should like to give your children some time in my realm. If that's all right with you." He said it was. Sean said he'd ask Rachel, but he didn't think she'd have any trouble with it either. "I've asked her, and she is all right with it as well. Jon and I are going to work on getting the babies we have fed. Thank you for telling him about it. I think this might work out well for both of us."

Becky came into the room with them, out of breath and smiling from ear to ear. She asked him if she was allowed to go, as well. Sean told her so long as they weren't a pain in the butt and that they behaved around Killian.

"We will. We're going to feed baby animals." She squealed, and Sean laughed. "Have you ever fed a baby animal before? I'm so excited I could bust."

Jon rolled his eyes at his sister, and that, of course, set her off. All he had to do was clear his throat, and they stopped. His dad used to do that when they were younger. To this day, Sean didn't know what that meant. But it had the desired effect. They, like his own children, had stopped what they were doing and paid attention.

After the three of them left, Sean got to work again. He didn't mind the interruptions as much as he thought he should have. Having someone come in and out seemed to keep him more focused on things. When he worked for several hours straight, he'd be sore and cranky about how his piece wasn't going as well as he wanted. He didn't have that problem anymore. At least not so long as the kids were around. Rachel too.

Putting his things away an hour later, he went into the house. There was forever food around now, and he was glad to see that someone was keeping the juices and other drinks stocked up as well. As he was sitting on one of the stools in the kitchen, Rachel joined him there. After kissing her on the mouth, a habit he was enjoying with her, she asked him when the kids were coming back.

"I didn't think to ask. I'm sorry." She said it was fine that she was thinking of taking him out to dinner. "Great. I'd love that. Just you and I? Or are we meeting the rest of the family there?"

"Just us. I wanted to talk to you about a few things." He said he was all ears. "I know. You listen to me very well. Even when I don't know what I'm saying."

"I just had a conversation with Jon. Or several of them, I guess. I think you're a piece of cake compared to him. He and my dad are just alike in that. People will think they're blood related once he gets out on his own around town." She said she was getting used to his dad's way of talking as well. "What is it you need from me, darling? Other than you taking me out to dinner?"

"I've been talking to the other women in this family." He said he was sorry. "They are a little intense, aren't they? But they were telling me some things I'm missing out on by not sleeping with you. Having, you know, sex and stuff." They both laughed. "I had no idea that you needed me to feed you from now on. I remember you telling me about it, but I wasn't really paying attention to your needs when I was bitching about what I was losing. Which, comparatively, is nothing. You've given up a great deal to have us here with you." He said he never thought of it like that at all. "I figured you'd say that. But I heard from one of the brothers that you're a loner and that it was funny to see you out with the kids, or even with me. I'm not used to being around people all the time, either. It took me some getting used to just to have my sister-in-law and the kids in my home."

"I might have been a loner, love, but with you guys here, I have certainly become very dependent on hearing your voices. I don't think I was so much a loner as I was a watcher. I love going to the mall or wherever and watching people just move from one place to the other. The way they interact with the people with them or the staff in the store." Rachel said she rarely hung out at the mall when she had shopping to do. "Now that you mention it, I've not done that in a while either. It's sort of sad the way the malls have become so empty. Anyway, anything else I can do for you other than get all spiffed up and go out with you?"

"Have sex with me." He dropped the little box of knives he'd been just about to put away. "I know that's very cut and dried, saying it that way, but I want you to have sex with me. A lot of it."

"I see. Because of the magic you'll get, or is it something else?" He didn't mean to sound hurt. When she looked at him, he could see the confusion on her face. "I'm sorry. I didn't mean to whine at you."

"I didn't think of the way that sounded. I'm sorry." She stood up. Pulling his stool out that he was sitting on, she sat on his lap, facing him. "I'm not sure of myself. Not like the other women are. I mean, just look at them. They're so buff and outspoken that I feel like I should just stand back and stay out of their way. I'm also not really sure how to feel about being your mate. I mean, do you get any kind of say in the fact that we're just supposed to be together?"

"I like the fact that we're supposed to be together. I love you, too." She laid her head on his chest. "As for you not being outspoken, that's not true. I saw the way you handled Charles this morning. I thought it was great how you just walked away from him without a second glance."

"I was afraid of puking on him." Sean laughed. "I wish

I was more like them in some things. Especially Jewel. She'll just tell you what she thinks even if you didn't ask her."

"You're more subtle than she is about that. All the women are dangerously outspoken. However, you are more of a just-putting-it-out-there what you think is going to happen, then walking away, kind of woman. They stick around to see the fear they've put into their victims." She asked him if they were victims. "That's what I think of myself when they're giving me a hard time. I'm an ancient vampire, and I'm scared shitless of all six of you. And Becky, too, for that matter."

They were still laughing when they exited the studio. He wasn't sure how serious she was about sex, but he was there for her when she was ready. Laughing to himself, he was thinking about what she'd say to him if he told her that several times a day, he needed to take a cold shower. And that his sleep was interrupted by dreams of her in bed with him.

Sean didn't care, not really. He was loving getting to know Rachel and the rest of his family. Not to say he wouldn't jump at the chance to make love to her, but he was all right for now. At least until he went to bed or had a thought about her warm skin. The way her nipples might look. Or even how she would look riding his cock. Yeah, he thought, he was so not in a hurry.

As soon as he entered the bedroom he was using until they were a couple, Sean wanted to sob. He wanted his mate so badly he was nearly to the point of begging her to touch him. Sean was in trouble here. Trouble enough that if he were to see just a hint of her flesh, he was going to come all over himself. Shaking his head, he dressed himself in a nice dark suit and decided he would work on seducing her. Tonight.

Chapter 4

She wasn't sure this was going to work, or even if he'd just tell her to get dressed. But Rachel stood next to the bed with nothing on but a smile. Not only did she feel ridiculous, but she was sure he was going to laugh in her face. When he came out of the bathroom, he just stared at her.

"Well? Say something." He nodded, then shook his head. "I knew this was a terrible idea. I thought I could seduce you, and then—" He was suddenly touching her. "I just wanted to show you that I could be pretty."

"You failed." Her heart hurt so badly she felt she couldn't go on. "You're well beyond pretty, my heart. You are the most beautiful creature I've ever seen. Now that I've seen you in all your glorious loveliness, I can't believe how long you made me wait to touch such a study in magnificence."

"I was terrified of disappointing you." He smiled and told her it wasn't possible. "You've been around for so long. You must have seen such lovely women in—"

"No. No, Rachel. I might well have seen lovely women before you coming into my heart. However, none of them were as beautiful as you are to me. You not only own my heart and soul, but I shall never look at another woman in all my life." Emotions like she'd never experienced poured over her. "I love you, Rachel."

"And I you, Sean." Sean picked her up. It was then she noticed that he, too, was naked. His body was chilled, making her shiver a little to be so close to him. "You're freezing. Are you ill?"

"No. I've not...there is no delicate way to put this, love, but I'm hungry. Not completely mad with hunger, but enough that I need what only you can give me." He nudged at her throat; she felt her pulse pound harder in her veins. "You're making me wild to have you, Rachel. To be inside of you is all I can think about."

"Take me. I offer myself freely to you." The bite wasn't painful, but it was a little scary. Almost as soon as that thought entered her head, she came twice as he drew on the wound he'd made. Even as he touched her body with his hand and fingers, digging deeply into her muscles, she felt his body warm, his heart pounding beneath her hand. "Please, Sean, take me."

He licked the wound at her neck and slid down her body. Each place he nipped at her skin, the more she wanted from him. The way he touched her skin was like he was afraid she'd break. Her flesh warmed considerably as he bit then kissed at her breast. Nothing could have prepared her for the meticulousness of what his touches did to her.

Her pussy was wet—Rachel could feel her juices as they ran over her legs to the bed. When he was settled between her thighs after pulling them apart for himself, she looked down at him and saw his cock.

Never had she seen one so full or so long as his. The vein that ran down the length of it was dark with blood. The tip of his cock was dripping cum as he shifted his hand up and down himself. Licking her lips, wanting to taste what he was doing to himself, Rachel looked up to this face to beg him for a taste.

His face was tight as if he was in great pain. The way his head was thrown back, it not only made the muscles in his chest expand, but the cords of muscles around his throat look sexy. If she could paint, or better yet carve in stone, this was what she would make. This man would be a carving that everyone all around the world would study.

He looked at her then. The eyes that stared back at her were red with their need for her. Sean's fangs were long and sharp. The thought of them sinking into her body again had her moaning loudly. Nothing in the world did she want more than for him to bite her again and again.

When he leaned into her pussy, she could only babble what she wanted from him — him to be inside of her one second, then for him to feed from her in the next. Fangs slid over her clit, making her come once again. Before she could catch her breath, she felt him do just want she wanted. He bit down on her clit, and she screamed with a release that made stars dance behind her eyelids, her throat raw with the scream.

Sean used his hands and his fingers to make her come over and over. One moment she'd be up, knowing she was going to fall. The next moment she'd be tumbling over a great vista; she knew only Sean could let her see. Feeling him feeding off her, drinking from her, she wanted him to fill her, give her more than she knew he'd given her thus far.

"Sean. Fill me. I need to feel you inside of me." He growled low, the vibration setting off an avalanche of several mind blowing releases that had her limp but needing more. "Please. I'm going to die if you don't help me."

He moved up her body as he had when working his way down. Little life threatening climaxes took her breath away. Sure that he was trying his best to kill her, Rachel grabbed a handful of his hair and told him to hurry. His soft chuckle should have prepared her for what he did next. Even as he slammed forward inside of her, she let go of everything within her until she had nothing left to give. Rachel slipped away.

She must have only blacked out for a few seconds, just long enough to worry Sean. When she smiled at him, he smiled back, then kissed her. The moment he moved inside of her, bringing his body as close as he could, she pulled him closer for a kiss that she hoped conveyed all the love she had for him.

"I love you." Sean looked at her. "I love you with all my heart and more. I love you so much I can't think of a word that would tell you that. I want you to marry me. I want to have a full long life with you. I want to spend the rest of my life showing you every single day just how much you've come to mean to me."

"I love you as well, Rachel. And I would gladly make you my wife. Today if possible."

She held him to her as he made love to her. Soft and sweet, he touched parts of her that no one had ever touched before. When he lifted his head and looked down at her, she watched his face as he came, bringing her along with him as the world shook around them.

When she woke up this time, she was alone in the big bed. His side of the bed was cold. Really, it occurred to her that she had no idea which side he slept on. She was right in the middle of the bed when she sat up and stretched. That was when she discovered she was slightly sore from last night.

Entering the bathroom to take a shower, she found the note on the counter. "Jon needed a ride to school this morning because he has a project due. Did you know he needs a computer of his own? We need to get them outfitted with that sort of thing." He told her he loved her. Then wrote something else. "You should know that I'm sore today. Like some woman met me at the door naked sore. I don't think I'll ever be the same."

Finishing up with her shower, she dressed herself as Sean had undressed himself last night. Going to the kitchen, she was greeted with a hearty hello and a large glass of orange juice. Not caring for the drink, she asked the cook if she could have anything else. The juice turned to tea even as she was asking Millie about it.

"The mister said for you to drink a great deal today. Also, he told me to let you know that the kitchen is magical. Anything you ever desire is in here. All right?" Millie smiled at her. "You're sure pretty. I know you know that, but the color of your eyes just makes me want to find your sire and hug him up."

"My father, he had the same color eyes. One blue, the other green. Jon also has them. Becky's eyes are green, with just a hint of blue in them." Millie said she'd noticed the girl's eyes this morning when they were having breakfast. "The kids are enjoying having you here in the morning. Jon told me that you give them both a hug when they're ready to be picked up by the bus."

"That boy, he sure does seem like he's starved for a hug in the morning. I tell you, whoever hurt them should be hunted down." Rachel told Millie she knew just where she was. "Oh, that's right—their momma. I'm sure glad you and his lordship are taking them in. Nobody needs to be that hungry for someone to love them."

"I agree."

Finishing up her breakfast, Rachel drank down another two glasses of tea before she left the house. She had so much to do today that she wasn't sure where to start. Just as she was getting into the car, Jewel and the other women pulled into the drive.

"You guys look like you're ready to take on the world."

"We decided that you're going Christmas shopping with us. I know you'd want to go with Sean for the major stuff, but we thought that having a day for ourselves, we can get things for our husbands they won't know about." Rachel thought about all the work she had to do, and it was Emerald that told her to just get into the car. "Tell Sean, you're with us. And I've already contacted the pack about the kids. They'll be there when we get back."

I was told to let you know that the women have kidnapped me to go shopping. Sean laughed and said he wished he'd thought of that. *Yes, me too. I don't mind shopping, but I don't know anyone well enough to get them anything for the holidays—just you, perhaps, and the kids.*

You know much about computers? She said enough that she could turn one on, then asked him about Jon needing one. *He has a laptop; both of them do. But he said it doesn't do as much as he wants it to. After talking to my brothers, I know he's right. I was only thinking of him looking things up. But with the two of them going to the pack school and the program they're in, they will need more than just a small laptop.*

I'll leave that to you and your brothers then. Unless one of these ladies know a thing or two about them. He said they more than likely did, especially Jewel. *I would guess that she'd be a little more savvy than the rest. What with her having her business running on programs to make the bags she's making.*

Jewel made gift bags that could be recycled into flowers once they were planted in the ground. It was a wonderful way to go green. Rachel wanted to do something like that while she waited on jobs from the FBI.

She realized it was quiet in the car and looked around.

"Where did you go?" Rachel told Mel she was thinking of something she could start working on. "I might have a project or two that you can help with. As you know, I can see ghosts. So does Ryan, but not like I can. There are times when I can't understand them because of a language barrier. I was wondering if you could do that for me."

"I would love to. However, I don't think that is going

to take up much of my time." Mel laughed and told her she'd be surprised. "I'm good with numbers too. Not like an accountant, but I can work around most issues. But I was actually thinking of teaching foreign languages at the school when the next school year starts up."

"That's a great idea. I thought of that as a job too, but can you imagine when a ghost pops in and has some questions for me? They'd all think I was off my rocker." Mel asked her if she'd spoken to Sean. "He's a wonderful person. I love him to pieces too. Like a younger brother."

"I don't." Rachel felt her face heat up when she realized what that implied. Of course, Mel laughed. "He's been so good to the kids. I think Jon would call him Dad right now. I know that they both think of him like that. And Becky goes to him with everything. Not that they ignore me, but I think just having a male around, one that isn't going to hurt them, has been good for all of us."

The two of them got out of the car and followed the others that were already hitting stores. She didn't know what she was going to get, but she supposed that didn't really matter. Rachel had few girlfriends, and she loved all these women. Not just because they were so unlike her, but they also seemed to be able to stand up for themselves without any problems.

Rachel was looking at the display of computers when something felt wrong, making her hair dance on the back of her neck. Turning slowly, she looked around for the source of her tingling feeling. Emerald and Mel came to stand next to her.

"Did you feel that?" Emerald said she had not but felt her

concern. "I'm glad you didn't say fear. I'm not afraid, not yet, but I am a little freaked out by this. What do you suppose it is?"

Emerald looked around when she did. It occurred to her that the cashier, a teenager she'd seen when they came in, was missing. Going to the cash register, Rachel put her hand on the counter to see if she was behind it when she saw what was going on.

"Mel, come with me." Emerald did as well, but it was Mel that she knew carried a gun. As soon as they were in the back storage room in the place, Rachel went to the closed office door and slammed her body up against it, breaking it open. "He's in the back near the safe. Call the police."

The young woman, her name was Holly, was lying on the floor. There wasn't any doubt she was dead—her throat had been slit from ear to ear.

Careful not to step in the blood, Rachel made her way to the back where the safe and the back door were. Not waiting for backup, Rachel put out both her hands and shoved them at the man. It took her several seconds to realize she was holding him about three feet off the floor. He was covered in blood. His face was masked, so she didn't know who he might be. However, she thought perhaps she might have an idea who he was.

"Christ. What are you doing?" Emerald was laughing. "So much for you not being like any of us. You hold him there. If you get tired, let me know, and I'll take him from you."

"I don't know how I'm doing this. Or, for that matter, how I knew I could." Emerald told her welcome to the family as she spoke to the police on the office phone. "Where is Mel? She should be doing this, not me."

"You just hang onto him, Rachel. Once the police get here, you can lower him to the floor, and we'll hold him the old fashioned way. But I do want to ask you, how did you know what he was up to?" She told him about the flash of the man killing the young woman and being in the safe. "By touching the counter, correct?"

"Yes. Is that weird?" Emerald said it wasn't, and it was, but they'd talk about it later. "All right. I can feel Sean trying to talk to me. I'm so stressed out right now I'm afraid to speak to him. Can you please tell him I'm all right?"

"I can. But he'll still need to talk to you, just so he can be reassured that you are indeed fine."

She nodded, and Emerald walked away. Mel pulled out her gun and aimed it at the man. Emerald yelled back to them that the police were there, not to move.

~*~

Sean had to wait until the police were done questioning the women before he could go to Rachel. Emerald had told him she was all right but stressed. Not that he didn't believe her, but not being able to break through to speak to her had scared him shitless. His brothers were with him now. Dad and Brandy were on their way in too.

As soon as he could touch her, his entire body seemed to go limp. If not for the chair behind him, he would surely have fallen with her in his arms. Sean looked her over when he had his strength back. She was fine, as she'd told him several times, just stressed.

"I'm confused about the girl." Her whispered question to him had him doing the same to her. "She was dead, Sean. I think she was dead even before the man moved back to the back room."

"Emerald brought her back. She said that no one should have to bury their seventeen-year-old daughter three weeks before Christmas. Holly was born on Christmas Eve, I was told, and her death just didn't sit well with Emerald." Rachel nodded. "I heard what happened. It's a little difficult to understand, as you've never shown that sort of magic before, have you?"

"Hannah thinks it was there all along. My mind just needed to be stronger, thanks to you exchanging blood with me, to be able to cope with the extra magic. I don't know. You'd think I'd realize something like that was lurking in my head. Don't you think?" Rachel shook her head as she continued. "Emerald keeps looking at me and laughing. Apparently, she heard me say I wanted to be like them. She might also be upset because she can't do this thing I can do."

"Yes. That sounds like her." Rachel asked him if they knew who the man was. "Not so far. They've not brought him out yet, so we're just waiting too. Whoever he is, the police are going to throw the book at him. They'll get him on attempted murder, robbery, as well as some other things I wasn't paying attention to enough to remember. Are you really all right?"

"I am. I promise you." Sean watched the comings and the goings of the police and other personnel. Jefferson was there with his team, as well as the medics that were taking care of Holly. She seemed as dazed about what had happened as everyone else was. "I knew before I went back there that he'd cut her throat. He told her that if she gave him the combination to the safe, he'd not hurt her. As soon as she told him she didn't know it, he murdered her. But from what I could see when I was tuned in to him, his plan all along was to kill her."

Jefferson came to sit with them at the little table he and Rachel were at. He didn't say anything, but he did hold Rachel's hand. It didn't bother Sean or his beast that another man was touching her, but he was worried about his friend.

"It's Charles." That was all he needed to say. They both knew then that it was hurting Jefferson in the worst kind of way that his brother had tried to kill that young woman. "Did he kill her, Rachel? I won't say anything, but I would like to know how far he was willing to go to rob that place."

"He slit her throat and left her there to bleed out." Jefferson nodded but didn't move. "I didn't know who it was when I went back there. I only saw that he'd killed her and was headed for the safe. I don't know what he would have done after that. I just knew he had to be stopped."

"I'm so very grateful that you did. Emerald told me that you took charge and went right back there." Jefferson looked around, then at the two of them. "He killed another woman earlier this morning. We found her body before we were called here. It was why we were here so quickly."

"I'm so sorry, Jefferson. I truly am." He nodded and continued to sit there. Sean understood. Since his brother was being arrested, he was keeping his distance, so there would be no one to say he did anything wrong according to the law. Sean asked him if he was all right. "I can take you home if you want me too."

"I think I'm going to be all right. Brook is here with her car, so she'll take me home. She was here when I arrived for the first murder." Jefferson shook his head. "He will be put away forever this time. Not that I'm concerned about his welfare all that much, but he is my brother."

"I don't know what I'd be feeling if it was one of my brothers that did this." Jefferson told him he had the best family there was. "Thank you. I do hope you consider yourself one of us. You've become a good friend to us, as has Brook."

"Thank you for that. As you can well imagine, I was worried that if Charles were to cause some trouble, it would reflect badly on me. It's nice to be accepted on your own merit instead of someone else's stupidity."

Brook joined them just as Charles was being taken out to the cruisers. He was screaming about his rights and that since he'd not killed anyone and gotten no money out of the deal, he should be let go. As soon as Charles saw his brother, he struggled to be freed so that he could get to him.

"Jefferson, you have to tell them to let me go. If I'm found guilty of this shit, I'm going to prison for the rest of my life. Come on. You need to do this for me. I don't want to have you come to see me with a glass panel between us." Jefferson assured him that he'd not see him that way. "Thank you. I'm going to be better. This is all your fault anyway. I told you I needed money. No one cared to invite me in for leftovers or even a warm shower. That's not right, and you know it."

"What's not right, Charles, is the fact that you can't get yourself into a position that keeps you from having to have a panel between you and whoever visits you. By the way, I'm not going to help you out, nor am I going to visit you in prison. I've washed my hands of you." Charles asked him if he was serious. "Yes. I've never been more serious of a decision than I am that one. You and I are finished."

Charles was dragged away, kicking and screaming for his rights. No one moved from where they were sitting until Brook leaned over and kissed Jefferson on the forehead. When they stood up, Sean and Rachel did as well. It was time things were taken care of, Sean thought. And he was going to do his best to make sure that things were working in the direction of getting his family safe.

"I'd like to speak to you about what is happening with Sandy Farley. What can you tell me that needs to be done to ensure my family that she won't be getting out to do anything like Charles did?" Jefferson told him what he knew, which was more than Sean had known. "I knew they'd exhumed Jonathon's body, but I didn't know about her parents. What do they hope to find there?"

"I'm not entirely sure. But when the courts found out what they found on Mr. Daniels, they were more than happy to sign off on anything your brother and sister-in-law wanted." Jefferson grinned. "I was told that if they wanted to end this, I was to assist them in any way I can. Even going so far as to order overtime paid to keep officers at the jail. In all my years as an officer of the law, I have never heard of that. It's like they're as afraid of her getting out as we are."

When Jefferson left with Brook, he and Rachel walked out to the car he'd come here in. Asking her again if she was all right, he didn't blame her for nodding, then shaking her head. He was sure that if he had to narrow down his feelings, he'd be feeling the same way.

"I want to pick up the kids, go to dinner, and then have some fun with them shopping. I know they want to get gifts for your family. I need this. Some holiday cheer." He asked her about the tree. "I'd love one in every room of the house. And if you ask, yes, in the bathrooms as well. This is our first holiday together as a family, and I want our home to reflect it. Let's go all out."

"Great. But first." He bent down to one knee and pulled out the ring he'd been working on for her. "I want to marry you as soon as we can possibly make it happen. I would also like to adopt the kids so they are Crosby children as soon as it can be arranged. I want the three of you to be as happy as I can make you and safe. I love you, Rachel Daniels. Will you marry me?"

"Yes." They kissed. Several people had stopped to watch them as he proposed to her. The applause embarrassed them a little, but he was happier than he'd been in a long time. "As soon as I can fix it, I'm going to take a teaching position at the local pack school if they'll have me. I'd like to teach language to anyone that wishes to learn one."

"Sounds wonderful to me." They walked hand in hand to the car. As soon as she was seated, he reached out to Joey, the pack leader, telling him they'd be by to get the kids. Joey told him he'd make sure they were ready.

Driving there, Sean thought of all the things he wanted to get everyone for Christmas. It was going to be a wonderful holiday, he thought. And they would only get better as the years went on. Sean kissed the back of Rachel's hand and felt like he was king of the world.

Chapter 5

Rachel was on a mission this morning. Not only did she have places to go, but she had a million and a half things to get ready for her first day of teaching. Not that she couldn't just make what she needed, but today she wanted to make her new room reflect the languages she was going to be teaching.

"Do you have any idea how that will work?" Rachel had been talking to herself for the last few days. It wasn't a habit she enjoyed, but she seemed to get more done if she listened to herself speaking. "Yes, because no one thinks you're off your rocker for speaking to yourself or answering your own questions."

There were two school supply stores in Columbus that she wanted to go to. Then she was going to go to find some books in different languages that she could have on hand. While she didn't think anyone was going to be able to read them right away, it might be something that they could look forward to. Or so she hoped.

"Where are you headed? And can I tag along?" Nodding at Jewel when she showed up at the house, they sat and talked for a few minutes while sipping tea and having a snack. "Where are you headed anyway?"

After telling her what her plan for the day was, Jewel leaned back on the couch. The woman was a thinker who had a good idea of what she wanted to say before she would let something terrible or painful slip out. When she was ready to speak, she would. But not beforehand.

"Did you know that your sister is going to trial tomorrow morning? They've found a jury here for her, and they're going to go on with it. I don't think this will be a short one either." Rachel told her she did know about the trial but had no plans of going. "You should. And you should go with Sean. Well, with one of us ladies with you too, just to show support. To show her that you just don't care what happens to her."

"Did something happen that you're trying your best to beat around the bush about? It's not like you to do the roundabout way of telling me something." Jewel told her about a dream she'd had. "You usually have dreams that worry you?"

"Yes. Quite often, as a matter of fact. But in this, you need to get with the judge about temporary custody of Becky and Jon while Sandy is there." She asked her why. "I'm not sure about that part, to be honest. Just that you and Sean need it for something important."

"I know, as a matter of fact. I don't know how you knew this, but just about an hour ago, the school called and said I need to get Jon's physician to sign off on some paperwork so he can play football. When I called the doctor, he said he couldn't do that for me because I'm not their legal guardian or their mother." Jewel smiled at her. "Okay, that's not exactly reassuring. What is funny?"

"As I said, I don't know all of it. Just that you ask for it. Then I woke up." Rachel asked if she woke up or something happened that woke her up. "I don't know what you mean. But if you're asking me if something terrible happened to wake me from it, then no. I just woke. Are you going to go then?"

"I guess I have to now." Jewel stood up, and Rachel did as well. "We'll have to work on this some other time. I wanted to get it done before school starts, but I guess it doesn't really matter. I won't have any kids until next week anyway."

"Would you like my advice on your teaching job?" Rachel didn't hesitate but told her she really would. "Good. You're going to do a lot of good with this. And making it oper. for anyone to join is going to be something that will help this town a great deal. Sometimes it's only the language barriers that keep people from finding a job. Also, having Jon and Becky there will be wonderful. They might learn a thing or two."

"Jon has been hitting me up to teach him German the last few days. He said he can take it as a class, but he knows that I know it. He's not so sure about the teacher." Jewel laughed and asked her what had happened. "Apparently, one of her students asked her if she could tell him how to say he loved his mother in German. When he said it to his German speaking mother, apparently it wasn't correct. He'd told her that he was a momma. Not the same thing at all."

"I wondered about that myself. A couple of phrases

she's used in talking to someone at the plant left them more confused than before. I don't use her anymore if I don't have to. Emerald is good at languages as well." Jewel laughed. "I don't think she has the temperament to teach a class full of kids. I'm betting if she did, they'd know every curse word there is in many tongues."

"Emerald is good at turning a phrase." They were both laughing when the other women joined them. She was glad now that she couldn't go to Columbus. This was better for her nerves than trying to do traffic. "We were just wondering what to do tonight. How about a nice dinner and some fun?"

They all agreed with her and started to gather their things to get ready to leave. The tree had been put up a couple of days ago, but there was a lack of gifts under it, as she'd ordered things online, and they'd not shown up yet. Christmas was still a couple of weeks away.

They were shopping locally for most of their gifts. She'd had to order a lot of her things online that the kids wanted because there wasn't a computer place ready to open just yet. Also, she'd gotten a couple of things like fruit baskets ordered to have them delivered to the nursing home, as well as the hospital. She thought it would be better than trying to find gifts for the staff there.

Rachel was debating about a comforter that she found when Sean reached out to her. He had been laughing, she could tell, so she waited for him to explain what he thought was so funny while she put the blanket in her cart. She moved on to the beautiful display of candles as he finally spoke to her.

I've just come from Jason's home. Did you know that he's been hoarding Christmas trees every time he finds them on sale? She asked him why he'd do such a thing. *He's donating them to the Salvation Army so they can give them to people who might not have one. They come with decorations and lights if the tree doesn't already have them on it. We have to do him one better.*

Laughing, she told the others what Jason had done, as well as what Sean had said. Then Rachel asked him what he had in mind to one-up his brother. She knew it was going to be epic. *We already do baskets to give out and gift cards for families in need. What do you think we can do?* He told her he'd been thinking on that. *Well, as you might well know, we're in town now picking up things on sale. Whatever you have in mind, remember that if it has to be wrapped, you're going to help.*

I love wrapping things. But that won't matter in my idea. I'm going to go and buy up a bunch of five-dollar items. After setting them up in the warehouse we have, you and I are going to make it so that kids with no or very little funds can buy something for their parents. How does that sound? She told him she loved it. But again, they were getting close to Christmas. *I think that is the only reason he didn't tell us sooner. So we'd not have time to make something better happen. But I'll get this done if I have to work all the time on it.*

The competition between the six men was legendary. Franklin had told them that if there was a will or a way for them to compete with each other, they'd have it going. He told her that she should just stand back and let them have at it—it was the best way for them to get it out of their system.

While they were still shopping, Sean kept her updated on

the things he was trying to buy in bulk. She thought him mad, but since he was having a wonderful time, Rachel didn't care. It was all for a good cause, and she hoped he'd be able to beat his brothers in this. Apparently, the other four were looking for their own ways of topping Jason.

While they were having their dinner, the guys joined them. Jason was bragging about how he'd been able to get fifty-six trees gathered up. Elliot and the others were saying that they had one better. She didn't know, nor did she care what the others might have. She knew that as long as there were Christmases and other holidays, the Crosby men would be trying to make things better for others.

On their way home, she told Sean what Jewel had told her. He didn't say anything for a few minutes, so she leaned against his shoulder. When he did speak, she thought he was upset with her.

"No. Why would I be upset about you getting one more dig into your sister? I just want you to not be hurt by her mentally. She's been trying that for a while now." That was true. Sandy had been telling everyone in the station that Rachel had stolen her children and had plans of keeping them away from her. "I don't want her to come at you with more lies and hurtful things. She's a terrible person and needs to have this shit ended by her going to prison."

"The trial is tomorrow. Overwhelming evidence was presented to the judge for the trial to be set. I don't know how she thinks she's going to get out of this. I heard she was looking at homes to purchase back home so she can live there with the children. What does she think she's going to pay for this house with? I'm sure she's going to expect us to do it if it comes to that." Sean promised her it would never get that far. "I hope not. Even to think about her getting out has me sleeping terribly."

"Emerald assured us that she'd never get out. I believe her." Rachel asked Sean if he thought Emerald would kill her. "I do. She knows what she's done to the kids and you. I think it bothers her on so many levels that she's still breathing as it is. No, Sandy will never leave prison. Alive, at least."

It gave her reassurance, but Rachel didn't want to drag others into her drama. At least with her sister-in-law. Hopefully, in the morning, she'd be able to get temporary custody paperwork so Jon could play football. Also, they'd be able to make decisions on medical as well as school things for both children. It hadn't been an issue yet, but she could foresee it coming around.

Tomorrow she'd go and talk to the judge and not say anything to her sister-in-law. Just nip it in the bud, she told herself, if Sandy started spewing her lies and insults to her. There was no reason at all for her to have to put up with her shit any longer.

Sure, she thought to herself as she laid down on the bed. Nipping anything in the bud that was about Sandy was a waste of time. Sandy didn't play by any rules but her own. If she had something to insult you with, even if she had to make it up, she'd use it. Sandy was a bitch, and she didn't care who she hurt to get what she wanted.

~*~

Going to the courthouse was not the way he wanted to

start the Christmas season. Sean had worn a suit and tie when he saw that Rachel had on a power suit. He loved the way the dark blue of the feminine suit brought out the color of her eyes. The way the different colors seemed to glow with happiness. The way her legs looked when she stepped out in those wonderful heels.

Today was going to be a telling day. A day that they get their lives on track and forget about all the other things that had happened over the long month they'd been together. That was his hope for this morning. Sean hadn't any idea why he was hoping for that, but that was his dream. To be able to get on with their life.

As soon as Sandy was brought into the courtroom, he could see that she must have lost weight by the way her clothes hung on her A great deal of it too, he thought. When they sat her down at the table with her attorney, she turned and glared at the room in general. Sean knew the exact moment she realized Rachel was there. He was glad now that they'd opted to leave the children in school and not tell them about what they were doing this morning.

As soon as the judge called things to order, Rachel stood up. Jewel had told them both to ignore Sandy if they could, except to point out to her that they were speaking. He didn't think that was going to work, but Jewel assured them that was the way to go.

"Mrs. Crosby. May I help you with something?" She said she had a small problem and that he could help her and her family. "I'll do what I can for you. Tell me what you need."

"Tell her to sit down. This isn't about her." Rachel reached for his hand, and he took it. "Rachel, where are my children? You were to bring them here."

"My nephew is wanting to play in spring sports. The school sent home some paperwork for him, insurance and stuff like that. He is also in need of a physical. Sean and I are unable to make sure he gets one before the season starts due to the fact that neither Sean nor I are his parents or his legal guardians." She asked to hand him what she had been given. After she gave it to the judge, Sean stood up with her when she came back to their seats. "As you can see there, Sean has put both children on our insurance. That was something that required more paperwork, but we're hoping that with some kind of note from you, we'll be able to get everything they both need to enjoy their school."

"I would imagine they're having a difficult time enjoying much of anything right now." The judge glared at Sandy. She started in on him being mean to her. That they were her children, and she refused to turn anything over to Rachel, the child thief. "You hush your mouth right now. We're not speaking to you. I suppose you'd rather they sat around just waiting for a word from you, wouldn't you?"

"Yes. They're mine, and she stole them from me." Sandy turned to her. Sean could see the hatred on her face. It was so strong he wrapped his arms around Rachel. "You're nothing to me. You never have been. I had everything under control until you had to stick your nose into everything I was doing. I could be out of here and rich if you'd not taken the kids. I would have made a killing in selling them off. I should have killed you like I did that stupid brother of yours. I still might have to do that when I get out of here. Jonathan was forever making me pay attention to those brats of his. Well, I showed him, didn't I?"

Sean didn't move. He had no idea what anyone else was doing, but he couldn't take his eyes off Sandy. She'd not only admitted to killing her husband but also her plans to sell off her children. Christ, he thought. She'd also said she was going to kill Rachel. When a movement out of the corner of his eye alerted him that something was going on, he looked at the judge.

"I want both sets of attorneys in my quarters. Now." He looked like he was about to have a stroke; the judge was so angry. "You two there, Mr. and Mrs. Crosby, come with us."

The judge started away but returned to pick up a stack of files on his desk. Sean could only read the top papers, and that was what Rachel had given him. After crowding into the room with the others, he stood behind Rachel.

"I think this has gone on long enough. No one is making any headway on this. Not to mention, the police officers where Ms. Farley has been staying are ready to quit. Hardened cops are going to quit their jobs over this woman." No one said anything to the judge's statements. Sean had a feeling this was the very reason Jewel had told Rachel to do this today of all days. "Do you see this stack right here, Mr. Marks? This is the paperwork that has been brought to me against your client. All of it has been researched to the hilt. Then on top of all this shit, she goes and confesses to several crimes that I'm going to try her for. What do you say to that?"

"I don't have anything to say, Your Honor." The judge

started to speak, but Marks cut him off. "You would not believe the things she's told me. Not about the cases against her, but just in general. Stuff that she wants me to do."

"Like what?" He said he wasn't sure he could tell him. "All right. You're fired as her attorney. Now, tell me what she's said to you."

Sean didn't think it worked like that, but Marks began telling them of the sexual nature of some of her demands. How she wanted him to find her a hitman for Rachel. Also, the man was embarrassed when he told them she was forever touching his cock.

"I thought about getting a plea bargain for her, but she absolutely refuses to think of anything beyond her getting out to her children. And the things she wants to do with them makes my skin crawl." Marks looked at Rachel. "She has a hatred for you that is scary. The things she wishes she'd done to you when they were all living with you are sadistic. Ms. Farley is insane if she thinks she won't get major jail time for even just one of the things she has told me."

The judge picked up the files and held them in his hands. Staring at them, Sean wondered if the man was trying to find some sort of divine answers. He was pretty sure there wasn't any such thing coming from the deeds of Sandy.

"I'm going to ask you one question. You can choose not to answer because of you being related to or representing this woman. But I'm going to put it out there. Mr. and Mrs. Crosby, would you be willing, right now, to adopt the two children of Sandra Farley? To keep them safe? To make sure that no harm comes to them other than normal daily things that children do?" They both answered him with a yes. "Good, Mr. Crosby, Mrs. Crosby, and Mr. Marks, do you have any objection to this family taking full custody of said children?"

"No, sir." Both Misty and Ryan said they thought the two of them would do a good job. "Certainly much better than they'd be if subjected to their mother," Misty added.

Mr. Marks didn't speak. Sean didn't understand that. He had already been fired from being her attorney. But when he stood up and sat down again, he looked like he was completely defeated.

"I think — and this isn't a reflection on either of you — but I think they'd be better off being raised by wild wolves than they would be with their mother." Marks looked at the judge. "I would also like to say that if given a real chance at making sure this isn't written down as a mistrial, the Crosbys have my vote in raising those kids. The only thing I would wish is that she gets the death penalty. It's too bad that Ohio no longer has it."

"Oh, good lord." The judge shuffled around on his desk for a few minutes. "Here it is. Because this trial was to be tried in Tennessee and had to be moved, she will be given the sentences for that state. Tennessee has the death penalty. This is from the sitting judge in her county. He said that if she is found guilty, we're to let the jurors know they can give her the sentence of death by lethal injection. They will carry out the sentencing when she is remanded back to Tennessee."

"I'm sorry. Can you say that again?" The judge repeated what he'd said to Marks. Then he handed the notarized copy to him. "This is something I'd never come across before."

"Me either, for that matter." The judge handed the paperwork to Ryan and Misty as he continued. "She just confessed to murder, attempted murder, as well as child endangerment. We have it all on video. I'm of the opinion that's good enough for a confession. I'm going to end this nightmare and have her remanded back to her own state, and not think of her again."

"I'm for that." He said that he was as well after Rachel agreed. "I would like to be able to go home and tell the kids they're not going to see their mother again if you'd not mind. I know they'll both sleep better knowing she's not going to ever be released."

"I'm going to do you one better, honey. I'm going to sign off on the adoption paperwork now that will make you both the parents of them and enable you to change their names. I'd like to think they'll be better off being Crosbys than Farleys at this point in their lives." It took him only another twenty minutes to have all the paperwork finished up. He even sent the courier to the courthouse to file the paperwork so that they could get started on everything today. "You two, you're going to be the best thing that has ever happened to them. Thank you."

Willie Marks thanked them as well. He shook Sean's hand and hugged Rachel. The man had never looked so downtrodden. When he started to leave the chambers, Rachel stopped him. The two of them stepped into the hall to speak for a moment. When she came back in, he could tell that she'd been crying. Asking her what had happened, she only hugged him. They were back in the courtroom ten minutes later, with all the paperwork needed to have Becky and Jon be their children forever.

Being seated again, the judge asked for Sandy to stand up. He wondered what sort of shit she was going to give the judge when she found out about her trial. When he and Rachel stood up when asked, the judge smiled at them both.

"After careful consideration, I've decided to forego giving the Crosbys temporary custody of the children of Sandra Farley." Sandy actually did a little jig before flipping them off with both hands. "I have decided that in the best interest of the children, I'm granting full custody of them as of today. The paperwork has been filed and notarized. There will be no more—"

"Wait one fucking minute. You can't do that. She can't have them." The judge, ignoring Sandy, went on to say how they'd be able to change their names if so desired and that there would be a payment each month for their care. "You'll take that back right fucking now. If there is any money coming, it's for me. I fucking birthed the two of them."

"Who was born first?" No one in the courtroom said a word to Rachel when she asked Sandy the question. "You have a fifty-fifty chance. Which one of them was born first? Also, what color are their eyes? You should know that one too, easily enough. They are, as you said, birthed from you. Answer those questions correctly, and I'll make sure that whatever money comes from the state for me to continue loving them goes to you. Tell me and everyone in here what you know about those two questions."

"You'll do that if I can answer those?" Sandy turned to

the judge and nodded. Sean wondered what Sandy might do with the money in prison, but then he'd never been in one, so he didn't know of what use money would be for her. "All right. The boy, he was first, and he has brown eyes. The girl, Becky, she came along later, about an hour. And she has them too. Just like her mother. See, I know as much about them as you do."

Rachel moved to the front of the dais and handed her phone to the judge. She told him that there were birth certificates in the file that she'd given him, and he studied them both. Rachel only looked at him, her face expressionless. When he laid the paperwork down, he looked at them, then at Sandy, before speaking.

"Ms. Farley, according to the birth certificates, Rebecca was born four minutes before her brother. They were delivered by C-section. Also, according to the picture I have right here, neither of them has brown eyes like you, but Jon has one blue and one green. Becky seems to have the same, but hers are both more bluish." She said he lied. "Why? Why would you think I'd have any reason at all to lie to you about something so simple as their birth order and the color of their eyes? I'm willing to bet that you didn't remember they were bore by C-section either."

The courtroom was cheering when the two of them left. The judge had joined them in being happy that the kids were going to be in good hands. Sandy was still bitching about the money that should have been hers when the doors closing silenced her. Sean pulled Rachel into his arms and kissed her.

"That was fun." She laughed when he did. "She didn't

know anything about them. I know the precise moment they came into the world. I was there when they were born."

She kissed him this time and smiled up at him. "This is a cause for celebration. The entire family needs to be in on this. And I'm going to stop by the shop and pick up a dozen roses for Jewel. She was right on the money for things to go the way they did."

By the time he'd been able to pick up three dozen roses, everyone was at the restaurant. He handed the first bunch to his lovely wife, the second to his daughter, and the third to Jewel. Becky was so happy about the news that she hugged the roses and him so much he was sure they'd never survive the ride home. Sean had a family. He was going to do everything in his power to keep them safe and happy.

Chapter 6

Jason didn't care for this part of his job. Not really a job, he supposed, but a leadership role that he'd gotten. Shaking his head, he wondered what the difference was when one of the ten men he was here to speak to sat down across from him.

It had been a wonderful Christmas. Now they were coming up on spring again. The time was moving much faster than it had when he was a man without a family. Now, it seemed like a day would pass, and it would be a month down the road. He wanted things to just slow down a bit. He glanced at the paperwork in front of him to bring himself to the present.

"It says here that you've been caught stealing blood from the humans." Bill asked him why that was a crime. "It's a crime because you know as well as I do that the rules were made up long ago, and we're to follow them. We do not take blood from humans without leaving them better off than they were before. We certainly don't take anything at all from the downtrodden. Understand?"

"I don't see what the big deal is." Jason just stared at him. "I mean, it's not like they have any idea that I took from them. I'm usually very careful about making sure they don't have any memory of me being there."

"That's the part that gets you into trouble, Bill. They usually *do* know you've taken from them. I have reports of eleven people going to their local police stations about being bitten." The smile wasn't improving his mood. "Look. You'll find these eleven people and repay their kindness to you in some way that they actually do not know it's from you. If I hear of you breaking the law once more, I'm going to have Emerald and her ice dragons end your life."

Shocked, Bill left him with several promises to behave himself. Emerald sat down beside him as the next person came to sit in front of him. He asked Sherry why she was taking liberties with the people she fed from. Liberties that made him slightly ill to think about.

"Sherry, you've been told several times that you cannot touch the human's pets after they feed you. I don't mean just touching, but you've been breaking their necks when you leave them. Why?" She told him she was old and didn't care much for animals. "Be that as it may, you are sentenced to work in the veterinarian's office for a period of ten years. If one animal dies by your hand again, either in the office or out, you will be sentenced to death."

Sherry glanced at Emerald, who smiled at her. When she got up to leave, he asked the queen of dragons what she was there for. Her laughter scared three of the vampires enough to fall to the floor and stay there.

"I love to watch you work. Not to mention, I think it will help them behave when they can see that I'm right here beside you. Also, I have a question for you." He looked down at the paperwork in front of him and saw this was more of the same shit. Jason called Carl to have a seat. "Also, two of the people here are going to die today, and I thought I'd just come around and help you out with that right now. I'm sort of putting the fear of me into them too. It's fun."

"I'm sure it is. Carl, you're here before me because you've been stealing money from the banks around the state. There is zero tolerance for that." He nodded and said it was fun. "No, it's not fun. It's theft. Today is your final day. Make your peace with your—"

"No. I don't want to be killed by her." Jason said that was the rule. "I don't like those rules. I know I have to die today, but there isn't any reason for me to be frozen, then knocked around like nothing to break me down. No. I'd rather meet the sun."

With a snap of Jason's fingers, sunlight streamed into the dark room he'd been using and hit Carl on the head. Within seconds not only had Carl met his punishment, but he was also no longer an issue for him.

Jason had no guilt, nor did he feel like he should give his kiss a second chance at their crimes. The people in his area had been getting away with a great many things for far too long, and he was putting a stop to that. Even with having Emerald around, he knew some of them were never going to stop what they'd been getting away with for centuries.

The next couple were the two that Emerald was going to

end.

"Margaret and Goebel, you are here before me for the crime of killing seventy-four humans for no other reason than you could. You've been found guilty by this court and will have your lives ended. The manner in which you die is not up to you but Emerald, queen of the dragons." Emerald stood up and became the scariest creature he'd ever seen, her dragons a close second. "All your worldly goods have been taken and divided up between the families of the children you murdered. Your names will be stricken from the books. You will no longer be remembered when the dead among us are counted."

The couple could not speak. When they'd been put into a cell, their mouths were removed so they could no longer feed from each other. The simple fact was that the two of them had slaughtered more humans than he had an accounting for, and he wanted them ended.

Emerald called her dragons as soon as she stood up. The room was large enough to hold the people—however, it was cramped when the dragons grew to their dangerous sizes. But Jason could see that the point was made just how she'd predicted. They would know he wasn't one to fuck with when it came to breaking the laws of their kind.

"Margaret and Goebel, you are hereby sentenced by your leader, Jason Crosby, to death by dragon. You will have no last words." Emerald put out her hand, and Jason watched, along with the other vampires, as the couple was frozen in place by the slow moving ice that Emerald was killing them with. When they were solid ice, she turned to her dragons.

"Destroy them."

No one moved when the great tails of the dragons shattered the two iced people. Jason looked down at his notes to give himself a few seconds to deal with the deaths. Not so much the deaths of the two, but the look of the bodies, broken into smaller pieces that still held the bones and other parts in small separate pieces.

The rest of the morning went quickly. He did have to use Emerald once more when Sherry, upon leaving the area, killed not just one small dog that she came across but also a herd of cattle that had simply been grazing in a field she'd gone by.

Gathering up his notes on the day, he sat at the desk he'd been using for the last few months. Jason asked Emerald what she needed from him. When she didn't speak, he turned and looked at her. Something was up, and he honestly didn't think he could deal with anything more today. For the rest of the week, he thought.

"You're fucking stressed out." Jason just snorted at her. "I was going to ask you if you'd watch the twins for us, but I really don't think you could enjoy having them around."

"Yes." She looked at him with a cocked head. "Yes, I'd love to watch the twins. Please. All I can think about is having our child. I think that if I get on the Internet once more to buy something for it, Jewel is going to have me committed. It might do us both some good."

"Yeah, she told me you were going nuts with online shopping. Did you really buy your unborn child a rocking horse?" He nodded. "Christ, Jason, it won't be able to ride it for about three or four years."

"It was on sale." It hadn't been. He'd been sticking with that story since he purchased it. It didn't seem to him that Emerald believed him any more than Jewel had. "Besides, it's a good investment, I think. Someday our grandchildren will want to ride it."

"Yes, of course, that's a good reason. You're a sap." He didn't even try denying it. "Chase and I have two meetings we're going to attend in the morning. I could leave them with the nanny tonight, but I think you'd have a good deal more fun with them than she will. Not that she's mean to them, but she's a bitter old woman that thinks I'm too hard on my babies. Just because I won't pick them up every time they make a noise."

Jason kept his mouth shut. He had seen both her and Chase pick up their babies and cuddle them when all they'd done was open their eyes from a nap. He supposed he'd be the same way. However, he was going to do it when there was no one around to catch him at it.

Going home, he reached out to Jewel to tell her what they were doing tonight. He was highly insulted when she asked him if he was planning to kidnap the babies so they could try out all the shit he'd picked up *on sale*.

No. I promise you that we're supposed to watch them tonight. He tried hard not to sound hurt by her, but she figured it out and told him she was sorry. *It's all right. I've never been a dad before, so I'm just having a little fun.*

Yes, but your fun is making it so I can't go buy things. You're hogging up all the new things I want to do for our baby. He'd not thought of that. Jason told her he was sorry as he entered the front door. "I appreciate that, but it's doubtful you're going to stop."

"Probably not. But I won't buy everything that catches my attention. I promise."

They were both still laughing about things they had yet to buy when Emerald and Chase came in with the babies. They were beautiful—the little girl and boy looked a great deal like their father. But Jason knew that even at six months old, they were more powerful than he was. And more so than he'd ever be.

When the other couple left, he and Jewel sat down on the couch to play with the children. They were just getting to the point where they would look at you and smile. He loved playing peek-a-boo with them and felt less stressed when they both fell asleep after having their bottles.

"You look better." He nodded at Jewel and told her he needed this. "I can tell. I'm having fun too. You've been so cranky. Lately, I thought that I was going to have to knock you around again."

"I'll never live that down, will I?" She shook her head at him. "I was a monster. I hurt you and a lot of people. Mostly you. I can't believe I'm still up and walking around after that."

"You're just lucky." She watched the babies as she continued. "I want so much for our child that I can't tell you how terrified I am about screwing up. I mean, my father was great, and how I wish he could be here to see all the new children in this family. But I also know that he's watching down on us to make sure we're not screwing them up too badly."

"You and I together will be just fine. We'll have fun too with the kids. I can't wait for grandchildren. Not just for my dad to have some around, but for you and I having a few. Little girls. I didn't think I wanted any daughters until I met you. I hope all our children are like you. Calm and even-tempered."

This time she snorted at him, laying her head on his shoulder.

He watched the babies while they slept. He felt his own body relax by degrees as they lay there, so still. Yawning twice, Jason felt himself drifting off to sleep.

When he woke up, he was still in the living room and alone. Stretching, he stood up and went in search of his wife. Jason found her in the kitchen with both the kids in highchairs, ones he'd purchased about a month ago. Since he'd not known what they were having, he'd bought one of them in pink, the other in royal blue. He was going to be all girly for his daughter if he were to have one.

They were making a mess of the room. He didn't have any idea how some cereal managed to end up in Jewel's hair, but she didn't seem to mind. As he walked more into the room, his bare feet encountered not just cereal but also a fork and a sippy cup.

"Can they use this?" He put the cup into the sink and rinsed it out. "I thought that once they're on a bottle, you have to feed them only that."

"No. I guess, according to what I looked up, they can start eating some foods if they want. I asked Emerald, and she said they'd been having fun with cereal. I didn't think she meant they liked tossing it around the room." Jason handed her a washcloth. "This is harder than I thought it was. You know, making sure they don't choke to death or fall out of their chair. It's terrifying having someone so dependent on you that even the slightest little thing can hurt them."

He didn't point out that he doubted Emerald was as afraid as she was. Also, the babies were immortal. Sitting down, he decided he might have to get a few books on raising children. Or better yet, have Dad move in with them until the baby was ready for college. He was never going to make it as a full-time dad.

~*~

Chase hated to leave the babies behind, but what he was doing now was important to a great many people. He stood up when Emerald sat down to get sworn in. Today they were going to be told what their new jobs were, according to the law of dragons.

"I went ahead and made you both a copy so you could read along as we go over them." Emerald looked up from the stack of paper that had been set in front of them. Mr. Hendel said it was going to be a long night. "Once we've gone over these, then we can go over the second packet of items you will need to carry on—"

"I don't think so. First of all, I can fucking well read. I'm not going to sit here listening to you drone on about rules when I have a copy of them right here. Second of all, no fucking way are you going to tell me what I'm going to be carrying around on my person when I've been doing this since well before you were born." Mr. Hendel told her this was important. "Of course, it is. I'm well aware of how important my job is. You just sit your ass right there and let me have a look at some of— There are four hundred and sixty rules here. What the fuck are you trying to do to me, have me get harmed while I'm trying to figure out what rules I need to follow? What the hell was wrong with the way I'd been doing it all along?"

Chase didn't bother trying to interject anything into the conversation. Emerald would either kill the man or leave. Either option was all right with him. They'd been summoned here by this man three days ago, and he wouldn't tell them why they had to go to him. More than likely because he knew this was going to happen—that the two of them would shoot him down on each one of the rules.

"This rule right here, the very first one you have listed. That's not ever going to work for me. I'm not going to ask them if they want a second chance in whatever they're doing. If they fuck up bad enough that I have to be called in, they've already fucked up any chances of a second or even third go round. If you fuck up, you're as good as dead if I come to find you." He asked what if she had the wrong person. "I won't. I can go through your mind without a second's hesitation to determine what crimes you've been committing. There is no way I'm going to miss something that way."

They were at the bottom of the first page when Emerald tossed the copy of the rules back at Hendel. She told him she wasn't going to sign off on anything written there. Nor was she going to keep tabs on those that wanted a second chance, and she certainly wasn't going to bring each person she was to kill to him so he could interview them.

"Why not? Tell me how you would handle things if the person had a just reason for whatever they'd done. Would you just end their lives without a second thought?" She nodded at the man, and Chase started to laugh. "Young man, I don't think this is the least bit funny. We're putting these rules in place, so there is fairness for all creatures."

"What is funny is that you seriously think either one of us is going to do anything in this book of rules. As Emerald told you, we're not going to be second guessing ourselves when it comes to destroying creatures that might well be waiting for the opportunity to do it again." Chase leaned back in his seat. "What if this person was a killer? Someone that told us they'd have no trouble following the rules from now on. We leave and let him go on living. Then, the very next night, he breaks into your home and murders you and your entire family. What kind of rules do you think we should make available then?"

"I have guards around my home so that no one can enter." Chase nodded, then went to the man's house and brought his daughter to the meeting, all within a blink of an eye. "How the hell did you do that? I should have you shot. That's my daughter you have there."

"So it is. I didn't encounter a single guard when I popped into her bedroom. No one was any the wiser when I put a spell on her to sleep. I was even able to walk out of her bedroom and disappear without causing a single alarm." Chase sat back down. "However, if you threaten me again, I will rip you apart. I'm not one to be fucking with."

"This is getting out of control. I have these rules here that you're going to follow." The books disappeared. Even the desk that Hendel was sitting at was gone. "What is the meaning of this? Bring those things back to me."

"Nope. I'm just showing you that no matter what you put before me, we can make it disappear without a single trace." Emerald smiled at him. "That includes you, in the event you didn't know. Who is this "we" you keep referring to? And if there is a committee we're supposed to answer to, then why weren't we made aware of it before I was dragged out of my home to come here to listen to you bitching about rules?"

"Everyone needs rules. What would this world be without them?" She told him that rules were good, but not for someone carrying out the law. "So, you're going to just go about your business as if no one is out there to curb your killing off people?"

"Yes." She stood up, and so did Chase. "This meeting is done. I'm not going to follow rules that I don't have a part in making. I do my job. I do a great job, and if you don't like it, then I can and will call forth my dragons and show you what real justice looks like."

They left the office then. Their plans had been to go to the meeting then have a nice dinner out. It was far too early in the day for dinner, so they headed out to the malls that were here. Being in a different city, they thought they could have a little bit of fun getting things for their children.

They ended up grazing their lunch meal. Emerald had never had cotton candy, and he fell in love with something called mochi, a ball of sweet rice dough covering a scoop of ice cream. He had two of them before he let Emerald have a bite of one.

Heading back to the hotel, they dropped off all their purchases and changed. It only took them seconds to do that, and they were out the door in no time. Chase had wanted the two of them to have some alone time for a while now, and it was great that they had such a good sitter tonight.

"Do you think they're having fun?" Chase asked her who. "Your brother and Jewel. I bet right now they're freaking out over some tiny little thing."

"More than likely, Jason is, but I don't think Jewel is. She's pretty confident in having kids around." Emerald nodded. "Someday, I'm going to look back on this night and think that you were beautiful. Then I'm going to tell you how much more beautiful you are now."

"That was so nice." She kissed him, and he lingered a little longer with her lips. "We're about to have company, Chase. I think the waiter is wanting us to order."

"I'm suddenly no longer hungry—for food." She told him she was and that he was to behave himself. "Party pooper."

They did order from their waiter, and Chase ordered a bottle of wine to go with their meal. While neither of them could get intoxicated, they enjoyed the taste of it when paired with dinner. Sipping his wine, he thought of what the future might be bringing them.

"There are times when I wish things were different for us. I don't mean that we'd never met—just different. Had I not been a dragon queen, I wonder what sort of things we might be doing instead of being hit men with dragons." He told her he loved what she did. "But I'll bet you'd be happier if I were, say, a nice housewife going to every meeting at school and making sure the kids are getting good grades."

"Where the hell did that come from?" She shrugged, and he laughed. "Emerald, you're my world, my everything. I was just thinking today how we have the best of all the world. Then I started thinking about our future. Do you think we'll be living where we are for the next hundred or so years? Will our children live close to us so we can pop over and visit when we want? These are just things that I think of when I'm working. I write them down, by the way, so I can see what came to fruition and what didn't."

"I saw you writing in it the other day. I wondered about that." He pulled out his worn notepad and handed it to her. She shoved it back at him. "I don't want to know. I want to live our lives like every day is the very last one. I know it's not, but there is something so profoundly wonderful about having no idea what tomorrow might bring. When I was a dragon rider, I only thought one thing all the time. To be safe. Or sometimes, not to die. But that's all I had back then. With the kids, we have now and the ones in the future, I'm set on making the most out of it."

"You're telling me to toss away my book." She told him no, that's not what she wanted. "You're right. I shouldn't be thinking of the future. I might get lost there, making things go the way I want, and forget about the things right here in front of me."

He tossed the book on the table and incinerated it with just a touch. Chase felt better already. Kissing Emerald again, he asked her how he'd gotten so lucky in mates.

"We both hit the lottery on that. I love you, Chase Crosby. I don't know why it took me so long to realize how happy I am." She laughed, causing the entire room of guests to turn to smile at her. "I nearly pissed myself when you disappeared and brought back Hendel's daughter. I think you scared him straight into not putting rules in place for us. Besides, I like our rules better. If you fuck up, you might as well shut up and take your punishment."

After dinner, they walked around the city. It was nearly spring now. There were sales going on to proclaim that the new fashions were in. He was glad to see sprouts of flowers beginning to peek through the dirt. The places where flowers were up and blooming made him think of new beginnings. This was his favorite time of the year.

After taking her back to the hotel, the two of them sat on the couch and watched some television. He did wonder how his brother was doing but decided not to check up on him. They'd be home tomorrow afternoon, and he could hear about their fun when he got there. Chase wondered not for the first time how he'd been so lucky to have his family close to him. Not to mention, just close altogether.

Chase did wonder a little about the future as he got ready for bed. There were things he still wanted to do with Emerald. Now with the children, he was thinking of ways to travel with them. To take them to places, he might well have had a hand in building. Even seeing things that were now marvels of the world. To him, they'd just been something new that wouldn't last, he thought.

Several times throughout the night, Chase found himself awake. Getting up when he was awakened the third time, he found himself in the living room again watching old movies, the kind that were brand new in his lifetime. There had been so many changes in the world since he'd helped his family save the queen of faeries. He wondered what else might be in store for the world before it was finished. More than he could imagine, he thought.

The next time he got into bed, Emerald spooned around him, then asked if he was all right. Telling her that he was and that he loved her had her getting closer to him. Once he knew she was asleep, he reached out to his father.

I just wanted to tell you that I'm proud of you. You took on a great deal in being our father. I love you for that. Dad asked him what had happened. *Nothing. I just thought I don't tell you that I love you nearly enough. I do, and I'm going to tell you that more often.*

I'd appreciate that. I surely would. They talked for a few more minutes, Dad telling him what his plans were for the day and Chase laughing with him. *I love you too, son. Very much. I couldn't be prouder of my boys than if you'd be in the White House. You think one of you might get there sometime?*

Why not? Dad and he shared a laugh, and Chase told him he was going to sleep now. *I'll see you tomorrow, Dad. We'll have dinner or something. All right?*

Yes. That sounds good.

Dad said he loved him very much, and they closed the connection. When Dad came back and told him to tell Emerald he loved her too, Chase thought it was the sweetest thing he could have done. Chase closed his eyes and finally let sleep take him under.

Chapter 7

Cody and Elliot covered up the last of the plants they'd planted today. There would be nearly full-grown plants by the time they were ready to leave tonight, thanks wholly to the faeries that lived in the greenhouse. It was the reason he rarely, if ever, had to order plants to fill the large nursery he and Cody took care of.

"Dad, can you tell me what these seeds are?" He loved being called Dad. It gave him such a thrill each time the kid called him that. "It only says seeds on the bag. I think it's from the queen."

One of the thousands of faeries came down and landed on Cody's hand. He was a great kid. Elliot loved him to pieces. But there were times, even after living with him and Misty, that he was still terrified of someone hitting him. As soon as he shook the faerie free of his hand, Cody burst into tears because he hadn't meant to harm the little man. It took several of them, at least a hundred faeries, to console him so they could work with him again.

Cody looked up at him. "I'm sorry." Elliot got down to

his level and asked him what he was sorry for. "For being such a pussy. That's what my mean dad used to call me. Aunt Emerald said he was the pussy on account he had to hit someone smaller than him to feel like a big man. But I still get scared he's going to come around the corner and take me."

"Cody, he's not. Not ever. And I'm sure that anyone in your position would feel the same way." He hugged the little guy, and they got back to the issue at hand. "I don't know what they might be. But they're large seeds, aren't they?"

"They're calla lilies, my lords." Rainy picked up one of the seeds and held it high above her head while she examined it. "Yes, this is a good seed too. Shall grow beautiful flowers that will brighten up any home with scent and beauty. I believe the lady queen has several of these very ones in her own home."

"Do you think they'd go well in here?" Elliot stood back and let Cody take over the conversation. He was getting better with speaking first in situations, more so every day. He thought working here was bringing him out of his shell.

Elliot went to find the other bags of seeds he'd been given to plant for the faeries. There were about fifty bags that were only marked with seeds. Some of them had hand-painted trees on them, so he just assumed they were tree seeds. He would have to try that. He'd not been able to put out any trees for sale because he'd only just opened up last spring. This year they were doing so well; it was the reason he and Cody were in here today, putting more seeds into the ground to have for tomorrow's business.

"Master Elliot, I was wondering if it would be all right if we were to grow more of the seeds in the back of the greenhouse.

There is plenty of room, and you have no one using it at the moment." Elliot didn't bother telling the young faerie, Pink, not to call him Master again. Instead, he asked her what she meant. Laying the tree seeds on his desk, she went right to them. "This would be wonderful to grow. Oh, my yes. These are fruit trees: apple and orange. I'm afraid that when they were bagged up, the person did not think to separate them into different fruits. So you will only know what they are if we tell you. That would be a good thing to put in. I've heard customers ask you about trees."

There was a tone there, one he thought was telling him he was being remiss in not having them already. Asking her what she needed from him to get started, she told him everything was in the back that would be needed, and she'd get on it right away. Telling her not to forget to mark what the trees would be, she nodded. He had a feeling he'd be asking them again for what he was tagging. They were always so excited to plant something. It mattered little to them what they were putting into the ground.

Just yesterday, he'd come into the greenhouse with lunch for him and Cody to find several containers of dirt with leaves sticking from the top of them. He didn't bother trying to figure it out on his own but went to find Cody, who had been there with him since morning.

"I didn't ask. One of the blue faeries came to me and asked if they could have some dirt. Since they mostly plant everything, I said you'd not care. You don't, do you?" He told him he didn't. "Well, when I went to figure out what they were doing with them, I saw the leaves. I just came back here to work. I'm not going to ask."

They laughed about that for the rest of the afternoon. As they were leaving for the day, he was asking Cody if he wanted to get some pizza to take home when he realized the kid was no longer behind him. Turning around, he looked at his son and asked him if he was all right.

"Dad, you have to come here and look." He was whispering, so Elliot did the same in telling him he didn't want to. "Yes, you do. You have to see the leaves they planted. It's...they're grown."

Moving slowly back toward Cody, he told him in the same low voice that he'd better not be joking with him. Cody shook his head, then pointed to the right. Elliot came around the corner where the leaves had been planted and stared at the containers for several minutes before he turned back to Cody.

"What are they?" Cody said he didn't know. "Do you think we should ask someone or just walk away?"

"If we walk away, there isn't any telling what they'll look like tomorrow when we come back. I think *you* should ask someone." He took a step back from him and smiled. "I'll be over here. You know, just in case."

Elliot didn't have any idea what the just in case meant, but he whistled for Pink to come and tell them what they were growing. The thing was, Elliot had a good idea what they were seeing, but it didn't freak him out any less. Pink landed next to one of the planters and smiled up at him.

"This is how the queen grows gardeners." Elliot nodded but didn't feel any less afraid of what he was seeing. "You can see that they're pods, can you not, Master Elliot?"

They were most assuredly pods. Each leaf had curled around what looked to him like a tiny head. The sparkles in the dirt around the leaves, Pink told him, was magic. He wasn't sure he wanted to pick one up and have a closer look, as Pink had suggested, but he did so anyway. As soon as he pulled the little container to his face, the leaf uncurled, and a tiny little body slipped out, naked.

His first instinct was to throw it away, as far and as hard as he could. But before his mind got in touch with his hand, the little person stood up, dressed magically, and then had wings sprout out behind him. Elliot was no less willing to toss it away, but then Cody was there, asking to see him.

Cody was a great deal calmer than he was about the whole thing. As the two of them stood there, all of the dozen or so of the pods had — well, he supposed, birthed. Each of them were bald, and they had the largest wings he'd seen on any of the other faeries. As soon as one of them landed on Cody's hand, he laughed. Christ, this was the strangest thing he'd ever witnessed in his greenhouse.

"They're gardeners." He told his son that was what Pink had told him. "Look. They have a backpack sort of thing around their waist. What do you suppose is in it?"

He started to ask if it was more pods, but he giggled instead. Cody looked up at him oddly but didn't comment. Elliot was freaking the fuck out, and he wasn't sure he cared who was seeing.

"They have all the tools born with them that they will need to do their job." Pink spoke to the faerie gardener on

Cody's hand in a language that he didn't know. "He wishes to show you, young Cody. Is that all right with you?"

"Yes. That'll be cool." As the little creature emptied his pack out, Elliot knew it was somehow enhanced so that it could carry much more than it would appear to. "Look how tiny that rake and shovel are."

Today there were more leaves planted and growing so that they could work in the greenhouse for him and Cody. Elliot found himself avoiding the area where they were growing for fear of seeing something he just couldn't handle.

Gathering up what they'd need to help with planting the trees, Elliot worked with Cody for only an hour, with the faeries doing most of the work. In no time, he had three apple trees, four peaches, and a lot of magnolia trees. He'd found out recently that Brandy, his stepmother, had a love for the magnolia trees. He and Cody were going to drop off a few of them for her on their way home.

Once they were in his car, heading home, Elliot realized that Cody was very quiet. He didn't intrude on whatever he was thinking about. Something he'd learned about his son was that he was smart and that he liked to have all his thoughts together before speaking. Elliot supposed that was because his father would have beaten him if he didn't get to a point sooner rather than later.

"Dad, I've been thinking about this for a while now, and I was wondering if you'd help me go to college." He didn't know where he was going with his question, so he didn't answer just yet. "I want to be able to be able to not just plant seeds but know a lot about them. My dream is to work in the greenhouse with you when I grow up. I love handling the plants and knowing what they are. It was really nice of you and Mom to get me that computer pad so I can look some of them up. But I want to be more than just a person working in a greenhouse. What do you think?"

"It would require a great deal of math, you know. Scheduling the planting to be ready when they're going to be needed. You just told me the other day that you thought you'd never use as much math as you were taking." He told him what Grandda had told him, about how there was nothing you could do that didn't require you to do math at some point. "He would know. Math is one of my dad's favorite subjects. He should have taught it, but he wasn't sure about being around a bunch of humans all the time."

"I've been working harder on math. It's not as bad as I thought it would be. I'm thinking I was just lazy about it." He had been, Elliot thought. His teacher had told them that Cody was much smarter than he let on and that he bored easily. "The teacher asked me if someone had finally spoken to me about my grades. I started to tell her that Aunt Emerald had, but they're all afraid of her now, so I just said my grandpa had. He did too, but Aunt Emerald said she was going to do something to me that would keep me standing for a year. I thought that if anyone could do that, it would be her."

Elliot laughed. Not so much at what he'd said, but how the school was afraid of Emerald. He thought that anyone with half a brain would be afraid of her, but the principal had sent home a note about not wanting to train, her words, any more of the Crosby children because they were all half-breeds.

He hadn't been there when Emerald had shown up unannounced. But almost the same day, there was not only a new principal, but also a new janitorial service, and several teachers had been hired. It wasn't just one person, he'd heard, but an entire staff that had been bullying the kids associated with the Crosbys.

"Okay. The teacher we spoke to at the open house said you were smart enough to take some college courses online if you wanted to. She did tell us you'd be able to test out of certain classes simply because you're much more advanced than any of the other kids in the school." Cody said he didn't agree with skipping any classes. "Up to you, son. But think about how much faster you'll be able to get to the goal that you want. Hannah and I only want the best for you. You know that, don't you?"

"Yes, I know that too. And I love you guys so much for everything you do for me." Cody told him what he'd like to do. One thing was to use his own money to buy himself a computer instead of a laptop. "I've not been studying that well when I'm at home because I can carry the laptop with me and go anywhere. I'd rather have to sit down and do it without moving."

Hannah met them at the door. It was the greatest thing, Elliot thought, to have someone there waiting at home for you. Going into the house, he realized they'd forgotten to pick up dinner, which seemed to be fine with them. They wanted to go and get some Chinese, something he knew they loved more than anything else. Except for him, of course.

~*~

Grayson watched Alex play the game he'd invented for him. It was a game that the hearing impaired could play, as there wasn't much in the way of talking, but sign language used all the time. It had been fun to make work, especially since he'd been able to put magic in the program that made it seem as if the characters were signing correctly.

Alex turned to him when another area was opening up for him. "This is wonderful. A very good usage of signing that doesn't make the person feel like it's a lesson rather than having fun. I think people will pick this up quickly and get a great deal out of it." He asked him if he could find any flaws in it. "No. But then I was having so much fun I didn't think to look for them. Thanks, Grayson. I think I can use this in my classes for teaching adults how to sign."

Alex was deaf since birth. But he was the most outgoing, confident person Grayson had ever met with a handicap. He would tell anyone he could that it was because his sister would have beaten his ass had he ever tried to get something out of life without working for it. It took Elliot a while to realize she meant things like food stamps, help with his bills, or anything someone more in need of it might not get because he'd gotten them.

Not that any of them had trouble with people getting food stamps or any other assistance. He was glad there was something out there for people to use. He knew firsthand what it could be like if you didn't have a pot to piss in. Grayson had been helping people out since long before this town was anything more than just a bunch of scrub and deer.

After making sure Alex had all he needed, Grayson went

to find his wife. Misty had been working on a big trial for the last several days. What she couldn't find, Hannah would. She was the best researcher any of them had ever seen. She found whatever she needed on someone, even things he was sure the people didn't know about.

Kissing Misty on the forehead while she was on the phone, he sat down in the chair across from her. When she hung up, she smiled at him.

"How aware are you that there are dangerous places to go swimming?" He asked her what she meant by dangerous. He was, he pointed out to her, dangerous too. "That's true. What I meant was, there are several places around the world that are posted and even fenced off that people shouldn't ever be wading in much less swimming."

"I know of a couple. I don't know that I'd consider them dangerous, but tell me which place, and I'll tell you if I've heard of it or not." She told him. "Honey, even from the name of the place, I wouldn't go there to swim. I take it one of the people you're working for has a client that went there."

"No. This is for a resort in the Dominican Republic. Someone's family is suing them for not having any signage to a place called Boiling Lake. These guys, a bunch of buddies, decided that they were immune to things such as signs and warnings. They actually snuck in, which right there should tell a person they knew better than to be there. But they snuck into the lake called Boiling Lake and decided to take a dip. It's fucking called Boiling Lake—didn't that give them some clue that it might be hot?"

"I take it there were deaths." Misty told him that only one

of the nine men made it out alive. "Christ, that must have been a nightmare to retrieve the bodies. How hot are you talking, just out of curiosity?"

"One hundred and ninety-five degrees. And they weren't able to retrieve the bodies. The man that wasn't killed is more than likely wishing he'd never heard of the lake either. He's lost nearly all his skin, as well as his fingers and toes. My contact person told me he was videoing the entire adventure when his buddies started screaming. He was hurt trying to go in and save them." Grayson asked what the lawsuit was claiming. "Oh, this is a good one. The families are claiming it should have been the resort's responsibility to make sure no one could swim in the water called Boiling Lake. And that the resort should have warned their sons to not go there. Here, have a look at the signage I got off an aerial view of the place."

Even he could make out the chain-link fence around the area. And it looked to him like there were danger signs every few feet. She also had a picture of the warning in the resort lobby that said that it was off limits to anyone.

"They're going to lose, I'm thinking." Misty nodded and leaned back in her chair. "Something is bothering you. What is it?"

"I would love to get away for a while." He said he could do that for her. "I don't mean a shopping trip, though I know we'll end up buying things, but just a place to go, hang out around a pool or a lazy creek, and do nothing."

"Camping?" She brightened at his suggestion. "I can make that happen too. I've actually been thinking about how much fun we'd have going camping. I'm not saying we should invite them, but your dad and brother have been talking about buying a camper for the last several days."

"We'll get one too. And if they want to go, they'll have their own sleeping place and camping place. Oh, Grayson, that's a wonderful idea. I can almost feel the nice breeze and the campfire food. Let's go as soon as this shit here is over." He told her she'd have to go with him to get a camper. "You go and get us something huge. Something we can keep for a while and have our children go with us on trips. My goodness, I'm so excited now that I could bust."

When he left her, he went to find Able, Alex and Misty's dad. Able just so happened to be in the media room with Alex, who was showing him the new game. When he told them what he was about to do, they jumped at the chance faster than Misty had when he suggested it. Since he knew next to nothing about campers, he decided he'd look some up before he left.

"No. That'll take the fun out of it." He asked Able why that would happen. "I don't know. But you'll have it in your head that you want this one particular camper and won't buy anything else. We should just wing it."

"I'm not good at winging it." Alex laughed when Grayson said that. "I've been a person who doesn't take chances on things that are going to carry around my family. You should know that by now."

"Yes. It took you four weeks to buy your wife a car. You're too set in your ways, old man." Coming from Able, Grayson thought it was funny. He'd been forever calling him young man since he'd met him. "We'll go, we'll shop, we'll conquer.

It will be the best time we've ever had."

Once they visited a few of the many dealerships around town, he was thinking this was a terrible idea. There were hundreds of different styles and shapes of the suckers, not to mention pop-ups, travel trailers, and fifth wheels. You could choose from the drivable kind as opposed to something as simple as attaching it to your truck and sleeping that way.

It was two hours before he found two that he liked. Grayson, at some point, had been separated from his fellow shoppers but wasn't worried. They could contact each other in a lot of ways, and he just assumed they were having fun too. But when Jefferson Quinn, the chief of police, found him in the showroom about to sign on the dotted line, he knew he should have paid more attention today.

"They've had your father and brother-in-law arrested." He asked him why. "I'm not quite sure how much of this you're going to believe, but they called us in on Alex first because he wasn't paying attention to the salesman. That was easy enough to clear up in my mind, but then they arrested Able because, and I'm paraphrasing here, he was knocking heads together. They used much more colorful language, but you get it."

"Does Misty know?" All Jefferson did was laugh as he nodded. "Oh, Christ, who do I have to pay off to get her out of jail too?"

"Nothing. I just came by to tell you that you're not going to be able to buy anything here because the name Crosby has been banned. Not only that...." He couldn't stop laughing. "Not only that but apparently you're going to be getting some hospital bills from when your little tiny wife, your very pregnant tiny little wife, hurt four of their salesmen when they tried to tell her to calm down. I surely wish I had remembered to pull out my phone for that. It was a treat I'll treasure for the rest of my life. You should have seen her, Grayson. She leaped right through the flipping air and landed on the first guy's back when he reached out to lead her out of the building. Then after that, it was a free-for-all of grown men trying to get away from Misty."

"How badly are they hurt?" Jefferson was still laughing when he looked up and saw his wife coming toward him. She wasn't just walking but seemed to be slamming her foot down hard enough on the lot that small indentations would be there for years. Grayson had a sudden thought that years from now, they'd be spraying off the lot, and they'd see the footprints and say to each other, "Ah, the Misty incident," and laugh a little. "Here she comes, Jefferson. You'd better not be laughing at her. She looks like she could take you on."

He didn't just sober up, but he also stepped back several feet. Grayson was both impressed and amused that people knew to be just as afraid of his wife as they were the rest of the women in their family.

"I'm so angry." He didn't bother pointing out that he could tell. "I've just spoken to Ryan and Jason. They're going to buy this place and have it bulldozed under."

Again, Grayson kept his mouth shut and just let her blow off some of her steam. She was still pounding the pavement, and he thought that term couldn't have been better demonstrated than what she was doing right now. Careful not to get into her way, he let her go and contacted his two brothers. They were laughing when he asked them what was going on.

We've not purchased it yet. I'm not sure how serious she was. Then when she told us to just plow the campers under with the buildings and people, we knew she was pissed more than either of us had ever seen her. He told Jason what she was doing right now. *Yes. Let her walk through it, I think. I will tell you what happened, as we've heard from Alex. Apparently, this guy was pissy anyway when he met up with them in the parking lot. Able had found one of the campers opened, and he, of course, walked into it. How the hell was either of them to know that it belonged to someone? It had only just been sold, and there wasn't any indication that told them that. When the salesman tried to tell Alex to get his ass out of the camper, of course, he didn't hear him. Then he suddenly grabbed him from behind, and Alex knew nothing but that he was being pulled backward. Fists were swung, and the salesman was hurt, badly enough that he's going to need stitches. Able was ready to pounce on one of the other men that had come to help the downed salesman, and that was all it took for him to start swinging too. They both were arrested and taken in.*

How did anyone know to contact Misty? I'm assuming it was her dad's call. This time Ryan answered him, saying he was called because he was their attorney. But Misty had answered the phone. *And she no doubt rushed down here to smack some heads around, and now that she has, she wants you to make sure no one is treated that way again. I think the owner is here now. Did anyone call him?*

I did. He asked Jason what he'd said. *I told him everything, including us purchasing the place and burying it. I didn't, however, mention that Misty wanted the people buried, their employees, too. He does know we're on the case of their company treating the handicapped unfairly. Also, there are recordings of the event, and it clearly shows one of his people trying to drag Alex out. I've seen them, thanks to their inventory being online. It was easy to hack into the system.*

"Hello. You must be Mr. and Mrs. Crosby. I'm Daniel Hawkeye. I'm to understand there has been a little misunderstanding about your brother." Grayson only had to put his hands around Misty's waist to have her calmly answer the man, telling him she didn't appreciate the way her family had been treated. "I know. I'm dreadfully sorry about that. If you'd like to come into my office, we can talk about it. I assure you, Mrs. Crosby, I have spoken to that particular man before on his behavior, and I thought after anger management classes, things were all right. He's been terminated." Mr. Hawkeye looked confused for a moment, then spoke again. "I'm not entirely sure why I told you that, but there you have it."

He did. Misty was getting quite good at making people tell her the truth without any effort on her part. Grayson thought it was what made her an excellent attorney when people were trying their best to get the better of her. She didn't use it often, but now, he thought, was a good time to know what was going on.

Mr. Hawkeye offered Alex and Able any camper on the lot if they would please not press charges. Neither of them wanted that, just fair treatment, but in the end, they did get a nice sized camper that even Misty approved of for half price. Neither of them wanted the man to come out a loser on this.

Misty was too excited to let one man make it so she couldn't get away for a vacation, and they browsed several campers that he had liked. In the end, Grayson and Misty were able to get exactly what they wanted in the way of a camper and paid full price for it. Since he knew how one man could really fuck up your business, he didn't want to take advantage of the man any more than Alex or Able wanted to do. Now all he had to do was find a bigger truck to haul it around with.

He had to figure out a lot of things on it. As they were leaving to get a truck, Mr. Hawkeye went over every detail with them, showing them things that hadn't been pointed out on the paperwork, and even laughed when Misty squealed a little when she saw how much storage they really had in the thing. Grayson couldn't be happier simply because Misty was.

Sometimes a smile from the one you love is enough to have a person leaping over mountains for them. Not that he'd had to do that today, but he felt very happy with things when she was excited to go camping with him.

Chapter 8

Ryan was ready to head out when his phone rang. Really not wanting to have anyone mess up his evening, he decided to let it go to the service. Calling from his cell, he told the lady at the other end he was going home. He walked out to his car and thought of nothing else but getting home to see Mel.

As soon as he pulled into their driveway, he knew that Mel wasn't home yet. Going into the house, he asked what dinner was going to be and decided he'd wait on her. One of her favorite meals was being cooked tonight, and he figured he could take her to dinner tomorrow night. He liked baked lasagna, but Mel loved it.

When she touched his mind, he felt disappointment all the way to his toes. She was going to have to bail on him, or she was being sent to some other state. He told her he loved her even before she started speaking to him.

I love you too. I'd almost be tempted to ask you what you did, but I know you better than that. What was on your mind when you said that? He told her about dinner and eating with her. *We can still have dinner together, but I do have to make a trip to Maine tonight. I have two I have to do for the Feds.*

They need to hire someone else. He knew he sounded pouty, but she laughed hard enough that he had to join her. *I've just had a couple of days packed into a couple of hours. Did you know that Grayson and Misty are buying a camper?*

I did. She told me all about it. It would be a blast for the two of them, I think. Travel around in such luxury that you'd never want to come home. I don't think camping is my cup of tea, however. He was glad to hear that because he didn't care for it at all. If he wanted to travel, it was to a nice hotel where someone else cleaned up after him. *Anyway. They're giving me permission to take you with me this time if you can get away. I will tell you that it will only be for two days, three at the max.*

I'd love to go. He did have a lot of work to do but figured that he could keep it caught up while she was busy. *We're not staying on site, are we? I hate that.*

Me too. No. When I told Ben you were coming with me since we had plans already, he said it was fine, they'd put us up in a hotel. I already upgraded it to something nicer than a room. Also, we're having dinner with some of the people working this case. I'm not sure what that means, but I told them all right.

I guess I can share you for one night. I'm going to have to work while you are. Mel told him she'd already figured he'd have to. *Great. I'm finishing up the last of the stuff Misty has been looking into for me. I don't think the case is going to be that difficult. It's pretty cut and dried.*

I was talking to Misty about it. Sounds like the men had no one to blame but themselves. He asked her how much longer she was going to be tonight. *Not too much. I do have to pack up some*

extra gear for this trip. After they told me what I was going to be
working on, I added a few extra things. I should be home in about
thirty minutes.

After closing the connection, he moved to his office after
making sure the cook was prepared for when Mel was coming
home. Burying his head in what he needed to work on, he
decided that someone would find him when Mel came home.

Instead of it being Mel that came to get him, it was Jon,
Sean's son. He'd been coming around for the last couple of
days to hang out. He said that his sister was boring. More
than likely, the kid was starved for male contact because he'd
heard from the others that Jon would hit their homes after he
left his. The kid had been abused too much, along with his
sister, and he understood quite well about needing to know
you're loved.

"I was talking to Dad about a couple of things. Did you
know there are over a thousand different kinds of faeries? I
thought there was only one, but apparently not. I need your
help with something if you have time." Ryan would do just
about anything for any of the kids in his family, going as far
as taking them shopping if they needed something. But Jon,
he was much too serious, he thought, for being just a kid.
"I'm going to write a book about being a kid from an abusive
mother. My life story, I guess you could call it."

"I think that's a wonderful idea, but I have to ask if you've
spoken to your parents about this." He said he had, but he
wanted to make sure he didn't get into trouble with writing
about his mom. "You'd have to get Becky's permission too. Is
she willing to do that? She can't sign anything, being a minor,

but she can give it to you all the same. I'd have to check about your mom legally for you. She would have to sign off on the story before you can publish it. If that's the way you want to go."

"I do. She's all for it, I guess. I sent a message to the jail where she's at, and they asked her about it. I don't call her Mom anymore, though." Ryan told him he was sorry. "No reason to be. I just call her Sandy. Rachel has been a better mom to me than she ever was anyway. Sandy is thrilled to know that someone is writing a story about her. I didn't tell them it was me. I just told them there was a person with firsthand knowledge on her who wanted to put it to paper."

Leaning back in his chair, he regarded the boy. "You're not as shy or reserved as you let people think you are. I think you get some of that observing people from Grayson. He could sit in a mall for hours and just watch people. I'm betting you do the same." Instead of answering him, Jon just smiled. "I thought so. So this book. You want me to figure out what has to be done, so you don't lose your ass over it. Is that about right?"

"Yes. It's going to be non-fiction. Also, I'm not going to change the names of the people involved unless it's important to their jobs. Like, I know that the Federal people are going to need to be changed. Since the entire world knows about Sandy now, I didn't figure it would take anyone long to put her name to it anyhow." He handed him a thick envelope. "I have these pictures too that I want to share. I've got to figure out how to blur some of the more personal parts, I guess, but they're from when I was living with Sandy."

They were devastating pictures, pictures Ryan would bet came from places Jon had been taken when he'd been too hurt to be ignored. Hospital pictures and pictures of doctors and nurses as they worked on their poor broken bodies. There were photos of his sister too. Flipping them over when he was asked to do so, Ryan saw that they were all dated with all the information on them that might be needed to look the files up. Ryan asked Jon if he was sure he wanted to do this.

Ryan watched his nephew as he sat there. He noticed right away that he didn't bow his head when he needed to answer a question anymore. Nor did he not look a person in the eye when he was being spoken to or even when he talked. He nodded once, then explained his answer to the question.

"Okay. I've been thinking about that question for a couple of hours. Each time I do, I think I don't just *want* to do it. I *have* to do it. Understand?" Ryan shook his head. "Yeah, Dad said the same thing. I have to do this because my sister and I beat the odds. I looked it up, Uncle Ryan. We should both be dead. If not for my new mom, I believe we would have been. We were victims. Not just of Sandy, but of the system too. I need to write this because I want to give hope to someone. I don't care if it ever sells that many copies. I could care less if it sold only one. So long as that one person finds something in it that gives them hope or help."

Ryan could understand someone's having to do something over needing to do it. He himself had those sorts of struggles daily. Looking down at the pictures, he wondered a couple of things. Why had these two survived? And where did the help they were supposed to have gotten fail them?

"Then I'd suggest you put something in it that has a list of hotlines at the back. Or better yet, something that will pull whoever from the depths of their pain to get out and find anyone that would help them." Jon told him he was working on that list too. "Good for you. All right. I'll do this for you. In fact, I'd love to look into this for you. I believe, as you do, that there are kids out there who might just need someone to show them there is a way out of the sort of situation you and your sister were in."

"Thanks." Ryan put all the pictures back in the envelope and handed them back to Jon. "I'm happy. I don't know why I thought you needed to hear that, but I am. In fact, I've never been this happy in all my life. I have a bed that is all mine. Food whenever I need or just want it. I'm safe. Also, I'm not stressed out all the time. However, I'm worried about Becky. I think, in some way, there is something deeply wrong with her. It's like more and more, I see her floating away. I'm worried about her a lot."

"In what way?" Jon shrugged and told him he didn't know how to explain it. "Are you talking something mentally? Or is it something deeper than that? You have to have some reason for thinking that. It's not that I don't believe you. You would know her better than any of us do."

"Both. I don't think she's dealing with anything in a normal way. I'm not sure she has for a long time. I thought she was happy, but I'm not sure anymore." He looked frustrated for a moment. "It's like she says the right things when she's around people, but when it's just her and I, I can see something behind her eyes that worries me something terrible. Like she's a big timebomb about set to go off. I'm not sure I'm saying this right. But I'm afraid of her and for her."

"Sean and Rachel, they have her seeing someone. You don't think this doctor is helping her?" Jon said he thought that she was too far gone to be helped by anyone. That shocked him. "Okay. I understand what you're saying, Jon, but what brings you to this conclusion? Also, have you talked to your parents about it?"

"I want to, but I don't know how to start a conversation with them about her. I mean, I have no doubt that they'll believe me, but I just don't know how to put into words what I see. It's a twin thing, I think. That I can feel her deeper and better than even Dad can when he can see into her mind. He's done that for me, by the way. The other day I mentioned that I thought Becky might need to talk about something, and he looked when she refused to talk. But it's there. As surely as I'm her brother, there is something not right about her." Ryan waited, thinking Jon had more to say. "I don't mean to say she's mental or anything like that. I just think she's not dealing with life. That even though we're both safe, she is waiting for something to jump out of the shadows and hurt her again. It's being raped the way she was. They took more than just her body, but a part of her that no one can see." He growled. "I'm not explaining this right."

"You are. As a matter of fact, I understand you completely. You should explain it just like this to Sean. Tell him I said it's like baby vamps that have been changed without permission, and they lose all their humanity." Jon said that was it exactly. "Good. I'm glad to have been able to help. Talk to them, Jon.

I don't want you to think I'm not worried, because I am. I've seen it before. Go home and sit him down and tell him what you're thinking."

After Jon left him, he thought about telling Sean what he'd spoken to his son about, then decided that Jon would do a good enough job. However, if he had any questions, Sean would know to reach out to him about them. The kid was smart. He'd do a good job of talking to his brother.

Finishing up his work, he got up just as Mel came into the house. Things were ready for them to have dinner, and after holding her for a few minutes, the two of them ate in the kitchen, a place where they ate more meals than in the dining room.

"I was talking to Jefferson today. He came by the office to tell me his brother is back in prison. I don't think he was telling me for any other reason than he thought I should berate him about not helping him more. Of course, I did pound on his head a little because he was feeling guilty. His brother deserves whatever they can punish him with." Ryan told her about the information he'd gotten. "I didn't know that they really have a commissary in prison. But how did they allow him to charge up so much without funds?"

"I don't know. I checked, and it seems he'd been in prison a couple of times before this, and his paperwork slipped under the carpet. They're going to make him work it off. In addition to him being in solitary confinement, he's going to be without even the most basic of needs until he gets his shit together. I don't see him ever getting his shit together for any reason. Do you?" Mel said she didn't. "Anyway, as to his confinement, they're also going to make sure he isn't able to make any phone calls or write letters. That was something else that happened while he was inside. He caused just as much trouble in prison as he did out, including murder. I haven't any idea why he was released in the first place. But he won't be again, I'm thinking."

"No. I've already decided if that happens, I'm going to hire myself a hitman or a vampire I know really well to hunt him down. He'll be toast either way." He told her he'd gladly do it. "I thought you'd say that. He's a monster and should have been put out of our lives a long time ago."

The rest of the meal was made with small talk. They talked again about camping, and he told her how dead set against it he was. Not that it mattered, he supposed—she was just as against it. There were people, he knew, that loved it—his brother was a prime example—but not him. He'd been a city boy, or some form of one, for too long to go back to sleeping in caves or falling down places to keep safe. Ryan loved the luxuries a hotel or its equivalent gave a person.

When Mel fell asleep in his arms, Ryan took his lovely wife to bed. She'd been working much too hard lately, and he wanted her to relax more. Going to his office again, he wrote an email to her boss, Ben Shore, and told him he'd like to request two weeks off when this new job was finished for his wife. Ben must have been sitting at his computer because he answered him right away.

She's been really running herself to death lately. I've been trying to figure out a way to get her to take some time off for a while now. Please, take her away and don't let her have her phone. I, as her boss, would appreciate that.

Glad that this was working out for both of them, he sat there long enough to make several reservations, as well as putting things together for some lovely dinners and a couple things they could see while away. By the time he went to bed, Ryan had everything laid out so that he and Mel could have a wonderful vacation. Maybe they'd not return, he thought with a small laugh.

~*~

Sean listened to Jon. He had come straight from Ryan's home and asked to speak to him. He hadn't any idea that the conversation was going to be so serious. If he was honest with himself, Sean wasn't sure he should be doing this without Rachel there. But Jon assured him that he would talk to her next.

"Do you think she might harm herself, Jon? I know you understand immortality, so you know that she won't die, correct?" He said he did, but as for harming herself, he thought she was already doing that. "Yes, I guess you're right on that. I looked the other day, as you know, and there didn't seem to be anything there that would have you thinking this. However, that doesn't mean I don't believe you. As I've told you, no one knows her better than you do."

Sean sat there, trying to wrap his mind around what he could do to help Becky. There were several things that he could do, but as her adoptive father, he was going to have to talk this over with Rachel. She might well have a better way to help her than he could. After looking at Jon, he figured that he needed to tell him straight up something that had been on his mind for some time.

"I'm not going to lie to you, Jon. I'm worried about her as much as you are. She does seem to drift off to places where I don't believe even you can reach her. I do have a couple of things I can do for her as a vampire. They're dangerous, as well as very difficult to do. I will do it, but I'd have to talk to you and Rachel first. I can essentially adjust around her ever being raped that day. I want you to think about all the consequences of what my doing this to her mind could be." Jon didn't immediately say yes, for which Sean was grateful. "There will be a blank spot of that time when it occurred. That doesn't mean it will be gone forever, however. What it means is just what I said—it's a place she won't be able to remember. Now here is the hard part. Something could trigger it to come back to her."

"Like, what can trigger it?" Sean told him it could be nothing more than someone remarking on her hair. Or something more horrific, like another rape. "I don't want anyone to hurt her again, Dad. She's suffered more than anyone I know."

"She has." Sean wished that Rachel were here. She'd tell him to be quiet and to go away. But this was important to Jon, and he was going to explain it as best he could. "She might well be pissed at all of us, especially me, if she does remember it again. I don't want her to do that, but if you and Rachel think it would help her out, I'm willing to have her hate me if she feels better about life."

"You're a good man, Dad. I don't think you get told that as often as you should." Sean hugged Jon tightly to his heart, where all of them had moved into as soon as he met them. "Do you want me to talk to Mom? I think I need to anyway. I'm not saying I'm all right with the erasing things yet. I think there is more to this than just her not liking you anymore. Isn't there?"

"Yes. More the process of hiding it than anything. But I want her to be happy. I don't think, as you said, she has been for a while." Jon nodded and sat back down when he did. "I'll work on everything I can think of that can go wrong. Because when you mess with someone's head, there are all kinds of things that can go wrong. That's something I want you to know about more than anything. All right?"

"All right." Jon sat there for several minutes without speaking. "I love you. So much, Dad. I don't mean just because you have the ability to help my sister. It's so much more than that. I also know that even if you *knew* Becky would hate you forever, no turning back from her pain in her heart, you'd still do it in hopes of saving her."

"I'd do that for you as well, Jon." Jon said he knew that. "How about tonight we sit down and have a long conversation with both Rachel and Becky. This affects her most of all, so we want to make sure she has all the facts beforehand. I won't do this to her without her permission either, Jon. It would be going behind her back on something, and to me, that's the same as lying to her."

"I thought you'd say that. I'm glad you think that too."

Relief like he'd never felt before rolled over his body like he'd been carrying a large weight. Sitting back, Sean watched Jon. The kid was only twelve, but he had the heart and soul of someone much older. Sean knew that growing up the way he had, without much in the way of help or love, would do that to someone. Thinking how he might well have grown up if his dad had joined their mother, Sean shivered at the thought.

"I'm going to figure out this book thing with Uncle Ryan. He said he'd look into what needed to be done so I can get it together. I've already started it, sort of."

"What do you have? An outline or something?" Jon told him that whenever he thought of something that had happened, he'd write it down and try to keep putting it in order with the rest of his thoughts, he'd been writing down. "That's a good idea. I don't know if I told you, but there was an envelope that came for you from the hospital in your town. Did you get it?"

"Yes. They're sending me copies of the incidents at the hospital. They actually called them incidents, like they were nothing more than boo-boos." Sean didn't dare laugh until Jon did. He knew he was serious, but he didn't know if he thought it was cause for laughter. Apparently, he did, and Sean marveled at the kid's ability to do so. "The information on the back of them is going to be a good way for the files to be pulled, Uncle Ryan said."

"He will be the best on the case to keep you from getting into trouble later down the line." Jon nodded. "Have you thought about a pen name? Or did you decide to go with your own name on this project?"

"I'm going to use my own. I thought about it a lot, mostly because Aunt Jewel told me she wanted to be able to show it to people and let them know that a Crosby was famous. I don't know about all that." Sean asked him if he'd thought about what would happen if he did write a bestseller. "Yeah, every once in a while, I think about it. But I can't get past anyone making fun of me as a kid, thinking that I know so much about being abused. I'm thinking, just from my own experience as a kid, that not too many even realize that kids have feelings and a mind too."

"I think you might be right on that."

Yesterday after talking to Jon, they'd set him up an account at the bank. Not for any money the book might bring him, but he had asked for one, so he could work and put money away for a car when he was old enough to drive. Becky had one too, but she didn't think she'd go to college, nor did she see herself driving. Sean figured she'd change her mind about that soon enough.

Jon reminded him again before leaving him that he needed to write down what might happen to Becky if he did this for her. There wasn't a great deal. Since her dying wasn't an option, mostly all that was left was how she'd regard him. What he'd said to Jon was true. If Becky wanted this, there wasn't anything that would stop him from doing it, even if it meant she'd hate him forever.

Sean was working on some of the latest contracts he had for his jewelry when Rachel joined him. She looked rested, for which he was glad. He thought her working too much and stressing about Sandy. He would be glad when her sentencing hearing was finished so she'd be out of their town. Having her so close had been good so that none of them had to travel too far on trial days, but it was wearing them all out.

"I'm supposed to line up three things for Sandy. She wants to see the kids—well, she's demanding to see them once more. I'm thinking that's a decision they need to make. Secondly, she is demanding money from me. The amount she wants and the amount I'm willing to give her are on opposite ends of the spectrum. The third thing is that I'm to set her up with a real attorney so she can get out sometime soon. That, my dear, isn't ever going to happen." He asked her if she thought the kids would want to go. "Five days ago, I would have said no way. But that would have been my heart trying to keep them from her. It's not my call at all. She is no blood relation to me, so I can't say what they're going to want. I'd just tell her to fuck off if it were me. But as I said, it's not my call."

"I think, and I have no idea why, but I think that Jon will say yes. Only so he can tell her off. He's getting braver every day about his opinions. I'm glad for that." He told her everything he and Jon had been talking about today. "So, as for Becky, I just have no idea. She's a complete mystery to me."

"When you told me that the other day, I started to watch her closer. I never realized she was drifting away from us. It broke my heart to see her so crushed." Sean said he was sorry. "Don't be. We're doing the best we can here, and getting her help and being there for her. And even though it's not enough right now, I have a feeling we're going to have her back with us soon. She's going to be all right. I keep telling myself that because if I don't, I hurt worse for her."

"I love you, Rachel. So much." She came and sat on his

lap, something they did a great deal. Sean thought Rachel thought he was giving her comfort, and perhaps he was. But mostly, she was sharing her comfort with him.

"I think we need to get all dressed up and go to a nice big fancy place and have a fun night out. What do you say?"

"Yes." Standing up, she said she'd tell the kids. "Great. I'll see what sort of table I can find us. Perhaps too, we should figure out a hotel to stay the night in that has a pool. Then on the way back through, we can pick up the camper. It'll be fun to load it up with the things we want in it as a family."

The camper was getting some upgrades in it. Mostly it was getting the things they'd been told they'd need to start out—blocks to keep the camper from rolling, sewer hoses, things like that. He was thrilled that his brother had told him what they were doing so they could be a part of the fun. Sean was excited for the kids to have some fun like camping too. He'd done it before, he knew, but it had been to keep him safe rather than just a place to enjoy. Getting things cleared off his desk, Sean was ready to go as soon as the kids came down the stairs. Apparently, they were ready for some fun as well.

Chapter 9

"Are you sure about this, Becky? If you have any doubts, we can wait for some other time, a time when you feel better about this." She shook her head, the tears that she'd been shedding earlier flowing again. "Honey, this is an important decision. When we came to you, we never meant for you to make it today. Just giving you all the pros and cons of it was my only intention."

"I don't sleep well anymore. I know she's in prison and will be for the rest of her life, but I'm just so terrified. Every shadow, even if it's during the day, I think is someone coming after me. She's a nightmare. Sandy is my nightmare." She cried a bit more, and Sean glanced over at her brother. He was trying his best to be brave; it was written all over his face. But this was his sister, and he was hurting for her. "Please, Dad. Will you please do this for me? It will be wonderful to sleep the entire night through."

As they prepped her for what he was about to do, he called his brothers to help him out. Not so much help, but to keep him on track. Sean was afraid, honestly. Afraid when he got to the part in her life where she'd been raped that he was going to lose it. He knew the men were dead, thanks to Emerald, but that didn't mean he was going to like it any more. They all, including his dad, agreed to be there for him.

When the time came for him to take care of the bad dreams and such, he went to find Rachel. She'd been acting tender since last night as well. Sean knew she hurt—he did as well. The thing about all this was that the person who had caused it all never thought it was that big of a deal.

"If I could get to her without causing any trouble for us, I'd kill her myself." Sean held her. "I'd not make it easy for her either. I'd just go in there and start chopping on her so that she'd fall apart before she was ready to die. I don't have a devious mind as Emerald does, but I think I could do some real damage to the bitch. I cannot believe she killed my brother too."

"I wish I could have known him. I'm sure we would have been friends." She leaned back against his chest, and he held her while she cried. "I'm so sorry you're hurting. I wish I could do something to take your hurt away too."

"I need mine. I need to let myself hate her. Not just for what she did to my brother, but to those kids. She could have destroyed them, Sean. If not for being immortal, I think Becky would have ended her life. Then what would Jon have done? He would have joined her, that's what. I hate her. I never in my life thought I'd hate that woman, but I do. With every fiber of my being."

"Sandy never deserved all she had. Not just you and Jonathon in her life, but those children." When she turned into his chest, he held her tightly. The sobs were making his heart hurt, and his beast roar at him to fix it for her. "I love you, Rachel. With all that I am, I wish that things were different for the three of you."

"Just help Becky. Please help her. I know there is a chance it won't last. I spoke to her just a little while ago, and I think this is as excited as I've seen her about anything." Sean told her that was good. "Thank you for doing this for her. Even in the event she does have it breakthrough, she promises she won't blame you. She even made herself a note. I know she was being silly, but she is happy that this might make her feel better."

After his brothers arrived, they all sat in the living room while he had Becky lay out on the dining room table. He needed to be at her head to hold her in his hands, but he freaked out a little seeing her laid out like a buffet. He was still berating himself for those thoughts as he had her lay on the floor. For some reason, he thought she liked that better anyway.

"Here is what I need you to do. Just think as much as you can about the morning of that day. You don't have to remember what happened; I'll find it easier if you just find me the day by thinking of as much information as you can." She stopped him. Sitting up, she turned to him. "You've changed your mind?"

"No. But if you don't mind, I'd like to forget the day before and after too. Sandy was hurting Jon that day because he wouldn't do something for her." She looked at her brother, and Jon just got up and left. "He wouldn't ask you to take that day from him, but it hurts me something terrible. Don't make me have to repeat it, all right? Just go there and take that from me too."

"All right." She laid back down and smiled up at him. "All right, honey. Just like I said, you remember as much detail as you can about the morning. After that, you won't have any thoughts that stay with you."

He moved to a position of having his hands over her ears. Of all the Crosbys, he was the only one that could do this. They all, as he'd learned over the years, had at least one very strong talent that they could use. His just happened to be removing memories or at least blacking them out.

As soon as she had the morning in front of her mind, he put her into a deep sleep. That way, she'd not relive it again. It was not just easier on her, but him as well. If Becky were to struggle through the dream, he'd lose hold of it.

As soon as he was able to enter her thoughts, Sean could see what Jon had suffered.

"You miserable fucking cur." Jon stood there in front of his mother. His face was bloodied, and she had a long ruler in her hands. "You fucking bastard. I wish I had smothered you when I had the chance. I want you to do what I told you right now, or so help me, Jon, I'll kill you where you stand."

"No. I'm not going there. You might be able to make me go by putting a gun to my head again, but I promise you this, that man will not survive trying to touch me again." Sean calmed his beast, telling him that he had this. "I swear to you, if you try to send Becky, I'll kill you. And you know damned good and well I can do it now."

All the hate he'd been feeling towards Sandy the last few days was nothing compared to the hatred coming from Becky. She was hot with it. A monster like thing rose up in her, and he feared she'd release it. Instead, she dragged her brother back to their room and locked the door.

"She'll just go get him." Becky told him to run away. "I can't. You know that. I won't leave you behind, and right now, you can't run with me."

It was then he noticed that she had a large cast on her leg. The pain was still there, so Sean thought it was a recent break. She told Jon she'd run later, but he wouldn't do it without her.

Just as they were making plans to leave in the evening, the door burst open, and there stood a large man with a ball bat in his hands. What happened next was almost too much, even for him. Sean had been to war, wars of olden time that were more savage than today's wars, he thought. But what was done to this boy while his sister was made to watch was something Sean hoped never to see again. The rape of him was bad enough. But the abuse he also withstood was sickening. Once the man was finished, Sandy touched the boy in ways that no mother, no one, should ever touch their child. If Sean didn't hate her already, this would have been the thing to solidify it.

What's his name? He heard Emerald there, just outside the circle of what was happening before him. *Can you see his face, Sean? Show him to me so I can end him in ways he'll suffer for.*

The man's face appeared, and he looked deeply into the man. His name was there for him to touch. His face would be nothing he'd ever forget, for he would be the only thing Sean compared all monsters to for the rest of his life. He stopped Emerald before she moved out of the memory.

You'll wait for me. It wasn't a request but a demand. He was well aware that she knew it too. *You'll wait for me so I can avenge my son.*

She appeared then, her face and body covered by her armor. The two dragons that were forever with her were there as well. When she looked at Jon and then Becky, she nodded once and disappeared.

This torture went on for hours. In the end, Jon was unable to do anything but curl into a ball. His mind had closed down. The beating of his heart, a sound so low it hurt Sean as well, was the only reason he knew the boy wasn't dead.

The day flowed slowly into evening. Neither child moved. There was no food offered to them, not that Sean thought either of them would have eaten. He could hear the sounds of Sandy, enjoying whatever she was doing on the other side of the door. Rage replaced any feelings the children might have had for the woman that birthed them.

Sean wondered how Jon was able to deal with the day's events. How he was able to be the one that— Then it occurred to Sean. Jon was braver because his sister couldn't be. Sean wanted to go and find the boy, tell him that he had so much respect for him. That he loved him beyond what a man would his son. Also, his respect for him as a human was tenfold what he had for his own father. And that was a great deal.

The next day started nothing like the day before. There was no sound coming from the other rooms. Becky got up and went to the kitchen. Sean had a feeling this was the routine they both knew well when they'd been hurt by their biological breeder. He could never call Sandy any relation to them ever again. Monster. That was forever what he'd think of her.

Becky gathered up two bottles of water, something in a pill bottle, as well as a sleeve of crackers. As she was sneaking back to her room she shared with her brother, a voice from the living room startled them both. It was the monster.

"Don't think that just because he failed to help me, you will too. I'm sick of the two of you acting like I'm not the owner of you. You will pay the man when he comes here." Becky didn't answer her mother but went into their room. As she laid the things out for her brother, Jon got up and helped her move the dresser back in front of the door. Sean wondered if either one of them realized the door didn't open the way they were protecting it.

The two children talked quietly to each other. He didn't know the time, but he figured it was well after lunch. Jon made the trip to the kitchen this time, and when he returned, he had the same meal for them—crackers and water. Nothing like fruit, which Sean had come to realize they both loved. There was no peanut butter, again something they both loved.

As he covered the memories, not taking them from her, he noticed their room. There were no games around. The beds, old mattresses on the floor, had no sheets. There didn't seem to be any pillows either. The room was devoid of things he thought of as childhood items—no stuffed animals. There were no books in the room and no shelves to have held them. It was a room, that was all. A room that was just as monstrous as anything else he'd witnessed.

They ate their crackers and laid back down. So far, neither of them had spoken about the day before. They never cried anymore, either. Even he had tears flowing down his cheeks at the thought of the things these children had endured at the hands of a monster.

When the door opened, the dresser they had in front of it fell onto the bed, pinning not just Jon but also Becky. As she struggled to get free, Jon was snatched up and chained to the floor. It was only then that Sean noticed the eye hooks on the floor at the bottom of each bed.

The man, different than the one before, shoved the dresser into the opposite wall. Becky tried to run. She went to the window to leap out. Sean could feel her thoughts—she was going to jump out so she could end her life rather than suffer again and again at the hands of this man.

There were three men that took Becky. There were no words to describe what they did to her. Rape seemed to him such a tame word for the horrendous things they did to the child. He thought she was not only brave to be able to live with the things done to her now but to be able to deal with anything thus far. To him, it was a small wonder that Becky was functioning at all.

Blacking out the day, taking the memories from her, he hurt, hurt in ways he thought he might not ever recover from. As he looked for references for the following days, he took those away from her too. Sean wished he could replace them with good thoughts, but he couldn't. They would be a lie, and he'd promised her that he'd not lie to her.

~*~

Jon sat next to his sister as she slept. He held her hand gently in his while he thought of the things he wanted to say to her. Dad had had a long talk with him, too, about the day he'd been hurt. Dad told him he'd never been so proud of anyone in his life as he was him.

"She needed me." Dad said he was still proud of him for being so brave. "I didn't want to be brave, you know? I wanted to die that day. A lot of days after that one too. I know she didn't want to remember that either, but I really wish she'd not told you about it."

"Why not?" Jon looked out the window of his room before answering him. "Jon, what was done to you, the things you endured, I don't think that was the first time, was it?"

"No." He thought about what he wanted to say to the man who never touched him with anything but love. It didn't freak him out as it did when others tried to hug him. Neither did hugs from the rest of the family. "She was forever selling me off. I can't tell you the number of times she did it. But I keep telling myself that had things not happened to me the way they did, I'd not be the person I'm going to grow up to be."

The two of them sat there for a little while longer. Jon wanted to just close his eyes and not wake up on some days. Today was one of them. He wouldn't. Jon hadn't any delusions that if he were to do that, he'd only hurt. Being immortal was a hard thing to have if you were just sick of being alive.

"I have an idea." Jon didn't want him to fix him too and told him that. "No. I'd never do that to you. You're right. You are what you are because of what you've been through. No, I have an idea that you and I should go and find the computer you want to use for your book. You have a good head on your shoulders, but I think you might benefit from taking some information from Grayson. He knows things about computers that none of us have ever been able to tackle. I was thinking the three of us could go and figure out just what you need to do this."

He thought that a great idea, then he looked at his sister. Dad told him she wouldn't wake until he let her. She needed this kind of sleep if for no other reason than to let her mind repair.

"She might need me when she wakes up." Dad told him she would forever need him. And that he and Rachel would as well. "Thank you for that. Sometimes I think I protect her too much. Maybe that's why she can't deal with this."

"No. That's not the reason. Like you, she's been abused more than most people have to endure in an entire lifetime. It's not that you're braver than her, son. But you're strong for her. Does that make sense?" Jon told him it did. "If both of you had fallen apart when you were treated the way you were, there is no telling how either of you would have turned out. Or, for that matter, if you'd have been able to live through it."

"I thought about it a lot." Dad nodded. "I could never make myself follow through with it because Becky might need me."

"And that right there is what makes you what you are." Dad laughed. "I cannot be prouder of you two than I was when I saw firsthand what you endured. You're a survivor,

Jon. Not only that, but you're dealing with it on your own very well. I think this book you're writing is going to not only be a bestseller, but I believe you're going to be able to help a great many people in similar situations. Some of them, I hate to say, might well be in worse situations."

"I need to write this for that reason." Dad agreed with him. "If you'll hold her here until we come back, I'd really like to go and do something fun. I'm sorry I didn't tell you. About the man."

"Jon, I want you to know that you can talk to me at any time about anything." Jon knew that and told him so. "Good. I've spoken to Grayson, and he is going to meet us at the computer shop in town. Then the rest of my brothers are going to meet us for dinner. He said he'd help you with it because he loves you. Grayson is the mushy type."

They were both laughing as they headed down the stairs to the car. Jon decided he was going to write down everything that had happened to him that day. His plan had been to make it just about Sandy and the things she'd done to him and Becky. But in order to make this something that could help someone, he needed to tell it all.

The computer store was overwhelming to him. There were things in it that he didn't have a name for, which he supposed was all right since Grayson seemed to know everything. The man really did know about computers.

Jon began to worry when the pile of things he was suggesting was getting huge. Grayson would suggest things he'd need and also told him of some things he could use but weren't necessary. Dad would pile them on the really expensive pile anyway.

"My thoughts with this are that if you have it, you can use it. However, if you need it and it's not there, we're going to have to make another trip with another hook up. This way, Grayson can get you completely set up on the first run, and you won't have any trouble making it work for you." Dad told him again, not to worry about the price. "One thing I've learned over the years is it's much easier to do a project when you don't have to keep going back to get the things you didn't realize you needed."

Uncle Grayson asked him what else he wanted to do on the computer. That was easy enough for him to answer. He wanted to be able to do his homework. Smiling, Grayson asked him if he wanted to do any kind of games.

"Like your dad here, I work on things easier when I have something around to distract me. Sometimes I might have an issue with one thing or another, and I find it easier to think it over when I make my mind blank for a few seconds. It will come to me while gaming, and you would not believe how productive I can be that way." Jon had no idea if that would work for him, but he was willing to give it a try. So, after returning the computer they'd already picked out, the three of them got one that Grayson could help him add onto as he needed it. It was going to help him keep writing if this book went beyond what he thought it would.

When they went to dinner, the rest of his uncles were joining them. Just to be able to hang out with them was more fun than he had thought it would be. They were huggers, and he didn't shy away from that anymore. When one of them patted him on the back, it felt good. Even when they leaned in to say something quietly to him, Jon never felt the urge to back away. He knew these men would never harm him. If possible, he thought, they'd die for him and his sister.

Dinner was fun. The uncles teased him as much as they did each other. Dad told him he was as bad as they were a couple of times, and it made him feel good. He loved being a part of this big loud family. He'd never thought he'd have a family like this one. Jon felt like he was part of something huge because of these men.

It only took Grayson two hours to set him up. In addition to the computer, printer, and other things they'd gotten, Mom had picked him up a larger desk to go with it. Jon was itching to get to play with it. Instead of asking Uncle Grayson again when he was going to be done, he went to see Becky.

Dad had taken the sleep off her as soon as they returned home. She was still resting, her body so relaxed she snored a little. Touching his hand to hers, he was surprised when she turned and looked at him. The smile she gave him was one he'd never had the pleasure of seeing before.

"Hi." He kissed her hand and told her he loved her. "I love you too, Dork. I feel so good. I must have needed this nap."

He didn't mention why she'd been napping. Dad had told him if she brought up what he'd done to her, then he could talk to her about it. However, if she didn't, he shouldn't either. Not that she might not want to talk to him about things, but just let her do what came naturally to them both.

"I'm starving. How about you?" He said he could eat. It

was a lie—he was still stuffed from dinner. But if she wanted to eat, he'd suffer through eating again with her. "You know what I want? You remember those hot things you microwave in a box? I want one of those meatball ones. Oh. You think we could have a meatball sub for dinner?"

He followed her down the stairs. When she asked about the uncles being there, he told her about the computer he was getting. Before they were on the last step, Becky turned to look at him. Whatever she had to say, he wasn't sure he wanted to hear it.

"I know something is different." He asked her how she felt. "Good. I don't remember what was done to me or why, but I feel different. Lighter. I don't know. Am I supposed to feel this good, you think?"

"I think you feeling good is always a plus. As for being different, that's all right, too, isn't it?"

Becky nodded, then hugged him tightly. When she took his hand into hers, the first time she'd done that without fear behind it, Jon felt like everything was going to be all right. That, for the first time in longer than he could remember, he had his sister back with him.

She had a whole sub made for her, and he nibbled on his. He wasn't the least bit hungry but enjoyed her company. Becky was happy, and he loved Dad all the more for it. Even if what the monster had done to her came back to her tomorrow, Jon would remember this day forever. His sister was free of it for now, and he was going to make the best of it.

When the computer was finished being set up, Uncle Grayson showed him how to scan the pictures into the computer. He told him that way, he could add them or take them off his book as he went. He also suggested that he put the information on the back of the photos into the computer so he could refer back to it.

"You talked to Ryan; I know that. But I'd send him the pictures so that he will have them as well. Backing up things is the most important thing you can do with this information you're going to be using. Also, I've set you up with an external drive to save things on. The computer will automatically send things to your computer, the external drive, as well as the thumb drive you can carry around with you if you go on vacation or something. You'll only need to plug it into your laptop or whatever you're working on away from home, and you'll be set. All right?"

"I love you, Uncle Grayson."

Grayson hugged him, telling him how much he loved him as well. When they parted, the big vampire got down to his level.

"You're my hero, Jon. I've never said that to anyone in my life, but that's what you are to me. Both you and your sister are still alive simply because of you." Jon told him it was both of them. "No. I don't think so. You are the bravest man I know. My heart will always have a space for you in it because of what you've done so that the two of you are here with us now."

Jon went to bed that night with a light heart. Things were looking up for them. He and his sister not only had a good place to call home, but they also had people that loved him, a feeling he returned to them. *Yes*, Jon thought, *I'm going to be just fine and dandy*, as Grandda said all the time to him.

Chapter 10

Harlan Windbreak didn't have any idea where he was. For that matter, he didn't know how he'd gotten there or what the fuck was wrong with his body. He knew he was chained up. Knew too that he'd been beaten up. The whys were just too many for him to figure out.

The pain in his head was making him too sick to look around much. There was a sound off in the distance that made him think of living in the state houses when he was just a kid. Smiling just a little, he knew that whatever reason he'd been put here, he'd be able to get himself out of it in a quick hurry. Growing up the way he had, it sure did teach a person how to keep themselves from being too hurt. Being chained up wasn't anything that was going to slow him down.

The movement just beyond what he could see clearly made him squint. Harlan wasn't sure if it was his head playing tricks on him or just the movement of a rat or something. He'd seen a few of them since he'd woke up. One of the nasty fuckers had been licking the blood off his fingers before he'd scared it away.

Bits and pieces of what happened last night had him wincing in pain. A man and a woman had tried to roll him — or at least that was what he thought they'd been doing. Usually, that didn't entail a person being chained up. They'd usually just take whatever valuables a person had and move on after beating the shit out of them.

The sound, like a scraping sound, had him looking hard again. There was something running down his head into his left eye, and he hoped it was just sweat. Harlan should have ruled that out when he realized the place he was in was colder than fuck. Blood. Whatever those two people had done to him, they'd beaten him up pretty well.

The sounds seemed to be coming from everywhere. The direction of them was difficult to pinpoint, as he thought they even sounded like they were coming from above. He wished he could just call out to see if whoever was out there would answer him. But he also knew, from his own experience at doing shit like this, that begging or even asking for answers would belittle him. When he had someone just where he wanted them, having them beg for someone to answer him would make him feel all the more superior to them.

"Do you really think you're superior to me?" The voice, like the other sounds, was all around him. He knew it was a woman's voice, but that was about all. "How does it feel to be chained in a room with a drain beneath you? I'm not going to tell you this to scare you — I couldn't care less if you're frightened or not — but you are where you are so that all your blood will go down the drain. Even after I have to spray down the walls to get the worst of it."

Harlan laughed. "You expect me to believe you're all badass? That you're going to hurt me in ways that are going to have parts of me hanging from the rafters?" She simply answered him, yes. "Yes, well, I've been torturing people for a good deal longer than you have. Also, it's been my experience that women just don't have the stomach for making someone scream. Unless, of course, they're a psychopath. Are you, little girl? Someone that enjoys killing begging men?"

"Psychopath? No. I'd say that's not what I am. I'm more of a…I guess you could call me a person who gets paid for making men beg. Also, killing. I've been killing monsters such as you for a great deal longer than you'd think." The movement in front of him was quick, almost like a streak of light passing before him. "Usually, the heart gives out long before I have the opportunity to get to the really fun part. It saddens me, really, that my play is only just beginning when it's over. But I've perfected killing monsters like you. I can make you suffer in ways that you just cannot imagine. Would you like to know why?"

The movement again, this time slower. This time he could see it was indeed a woman, and she was beautiful. Not only that, he thought her dressed all in glass—a trick of the lighting. Harlan thought she was all words and no play. He was rather enjoying this.

"Yes, why don't you tell me your little secret. Tell me so the next time I'm playing, I can do the same. I have found that sometimes I take just a little too long. Then I have to just end my fun before it really has a chance to begin." Harlan laughed a little louder this time. "Go ahead, tell me what it is you do to make the person live until you've had enough."

"I bring them back to life over and over with magic." He felt the slice through his throat, the warmth of his blood running down his chest. Coughing, trying to pull free of his chains, he knew she'd been playing him all along. Then she was there, right in front of him. "You see? It brings you back to me so I can continue for a little while longer."

She'd cut his throat. He knew he hadn't imagined that. Now it was as if nothing had happened. The blood was still there—he could see it staining his shirt. It was fresh too. Blood, old blood, would turn brown when it was sitting. This was as red as he had ever seen. Twisting his head, moving his neck just enough to wince in pain, he looked around for the woman. Her laughter felt like it was a part of the room that seemed to be closing in on him.

"I, however, am not the one that is going to kill you. Because, Harlan, I want you to have no illusions that you're going to walk away from this. I was told I could have my fun with you. I could even hurt you some. But you belong to another, a man that has pain in his heart for something you did to one of his." Harlan didn't have any idea what she was going on about and told her that. "I can give you hints. I cannot outright tell you who or what it is you've done. Though I've had a very complete search through that nasty mind of yours, and I doubt even giving you hints will narrow it down for you."

"What the fuck are you talking about? Why am I here? What is it you think I've done to deserve this?" There were several things that could have had him chained like he was.

Even more things he should die for. But he wasn't going to go down easily. He was a man who prided himself on having as much fun as he possibly could. "Where are you, bitch? Show yourself to me."

She stood in front of him again, not close enough to touch him, but close enough that he didn't have to squint to see her. Christ, she was beautiful. Her body was one that men dreamed of taking. Her face was one that he was sure graced paintings of goddesses. When she threw back her head and laughed, he could see that along with her beauty, there was also danger. Her fangs were as long as his fingers. They were also sharper than any knife he'd ever carried.

"You look like you need to have some things cleared up for you, Harlan. Let me do that for you right now. First of all, I'm not nearly as young as you might have in your head. I'm an ancient. Older than even the dirt beneath your feet. Stronger than the stone that holds up these walls around us. More powerful than an atomic bomb—any bomb, for that matter. I am, in a word, magic." She moved around the room with dizzying speed until he was sick with it. When she finally stopped, he couldn't have looked directly at her if she'd put a gun to his head. Closing his eyes, he heard the scraping sound again. Looking to his right, he screamed with what he saw there. "They're mine and will not harm you unless I tell them to. I would like for you to take note of their size. The manner in which they move. One breath from them—there are two of them there—and you will be nothing more than a block of ice. A block so cold and solid that only their tail hitting it will break through. Of course, you'll die as well, but that's what we're here for anyway, aren't we, Harlan?"

The two dragons moved around the room. They were large but not cumbersome. Their movements were graceful — like a pair of dancers, he thought. Harlan didn't know where that thought came from, but he knew it to be true. They might well be as deadly as she said, but right now, they were the most beautiful creatures he'd ever seen.

"You said you'd give me a hint." His mind didn't want to dwell on the things she'd said the dragons could do. Harlan was afraid that if he did, he'd think about dying. He wasn't going to. She was only telling him this to make him think he was. One of the oldest tricks in the book, he thought to himself. "What is it that has you bringing me here to put up with your bullshit?"

"A hint. All right. Here is a good one. What does the name Jon mean to you? Anything?" It didn't. Not that he'd never heard the name before. There were plenty of Jons in the world. When he told her she'd have to do better, she gave him a second name. "Does the name Sean mean anything to you? How about Sean Crosby?"

"Nope." He did have a little tickle of a memory of the name Crosby, but he was enjoying this too much to tell her that. This bantering back and forth, it was fun for him. He usually didn't get to talk to his victims. They were gagged when he had his fun. He might try leaving them to talk to him while he taunted them. "I don't know either of those names. How about you tell me what it is I've allegedly done to them? Then I can try and remember them that way."

"I think that is more than enough to bring you up to date

on why you're here. I will tell you that Sean is here now. I've only had the privilege of playing with you until he was free to come and kill you. Also, you might pretend to remember this about him, but Crosby is a vampire. A very old and very pissed off vampire."

"Vampire, huh? Well, bring it on, vampire. Whatever you think I've done, I'm sure you've done a good deal worse." Harlan knew it was a joke now. There were no such things as vampires. "You bring it on, buddy, and we'll trade ways of killing people."

The laugh made his balls tighten to his body. It wasn't a woman this time, but a man. The way the sounds echoed around the room made him think evil surrounded him. Not just that, but an evil the likes of which he'd never seen before.

"Hello, Harlan." It was an educated voice, with a bit of an accent he'd never heard before. Cocking one ear in the direction from which the woman had come out of the shadows, he wanted to get something on the man he'd bet no one had gotten before. "I think it's funny that you don't believe I exist. That vampires aren't real. It's a shame, really, that you're going to learn that not only are we real, but that we protect what we love with every ounce of ourselves."

"Hey, if I hurt one of your pets, I'm sorry about that. But a man has to have some fun, don't you think?" Sean didn't answer him. "I tell you what, Sean. I'll give you every penny I have, and we'll call it even. How about that?"

"Money? For my son? No. Nothing you have in the tangible sense interests me. No. You might say I'm out for blood. All of yours draining out of your body while I watch."

He told him he was sorry. For some reason, Harlan thought this man was serious that he was going to kill him. "I am, you know. Going to kill you. There is no doubt at all that I'm going to kill you slowly, too."

"Look. You can have everything. I have a couple of houses too. All of it, it's yours." The movement this time brought the man to stand in front of his face. Harlan knew in that moment that he was looking into eyes that had not only committed evil acts but perhaps had been the very reason for the word evil. "Please."

Harlan couldn't look away. All he could do was stare into the red eyes that bore into him. They were dark too, red so dark that it looked like blood. It seeped from them; blood did. The man was so dark, everything about him showing the darker side of him, that Harlan had to wonder if the movies had ever really seen a vampire. If they had, their movies would be a great deal scarier than anything they had ever produced for people to enjoy.

"I am here for this."

All Sean did was touch his forehead, and it was right there for Harlan to remember. The view in his mind was like a rolling movie. He knew why the man was there. Harlan even knew the name of the child. Jon Daniels. Son of Sandy Farley.

Harlan felt his bladder empty, his pants fill with a vile smelling shit that made him sick with it. But it was the rape of a ten-year-old little boy. The sodomy of someone so beaten that he remembered it as if he'd done it yesterday. He'd done the beating. Harlan had taken the boy over and over at his mother's request. Harlan not only saw what he'd done to the young child but felt every wound and deed he'd done to him.

Every time what he'd done came to an end, the vampire would slash at him, his neck, arms, and face. Harlan felt parts of himself fall from his body. Each slash would open new wounds that would drain him just a little more.

Sean never said a word except one the entire time he kept him alive. "Jon." That was all he said, the boy's name over and over as he cut more of Harlan's body away. Let more of his blood drain into the hole he had been told was there.

When the woman appeared again, she put her hand on the man, pushing him back against the wall just beyond where Harlan could see. Not that he could see too much. Harlan thought that at some point, he'd lost one of his eyes.

"Please. End me." The two of them argued. He didn't know what they said, their language beyond whatever he had learned in school. But they were angry. That much anyone could tell. "Kill me. Please. End me."

~*~

"Enough." Sean roared at Emerald, letting his monster inside try and hurt her. "You've killed him more times than even I have when playing. End him, or I will."

"No. He must suffer for all the suffering Jon has endured." Emerald told him to look at what he'd done. Sean was beyond looking at anything right now. His beast had taken control of him, and Sean, the man, was no longer there. "He must suffer for my Jon."

"Look at him, you fucking bastard. He's paid enough." Sean could feel himself being forced to the forefront, to be the person that would be there for others. When he looked at Harlan, his belly actually churned up. "You did enough, Sean. He's paid enough. Don't you think?"

Sean collapsed. He held on to Emerald as tightly as he could as his beast let him go. He'd gone beyond anything he'd ever done before. Not just for a vampire, but even a monster. Sean cried out his pain, cried for what he'd done to this man. As he sat there in the blood-soaked basement, he watched as not only did Emerald end the man as she said she would, but the room was once again a pristine place.

"Come on. You need to take a shower. I can't clean you up like I did the room. You'll smell like me, and that won't be good for either of us."

She took him to a stall, and he stood under the spray of cold water until the water no longer ran red. Then, when she told him to strip, he watched as parts of Harlan joined the blood as it circled the drain.

"Don't leave me."

"I'm not. I'm right here when you're finished." Sean pulled the shampoo off the shelf above his head, but he couldn't open it. His mind kept seeing the man he'd killed. "Don't, Sean. You did what needed to be done. You know in your head that the man deserved this and more. You can't let it get you down, or you're going to be as haunted as Becky is."

Concentrating on one thing at a time, he opened the shampoo bottle then washed his hair. No longer looking down at the drain, he kept his eyes closed as he washed his body. Even now that he was naked, there were still places where his fingers would encounter something foreign to him. Something that would have his mind flashing to what he'd done.

Emerald spoke to him from the other side of the now closed shower door. "Chase knows why we're here. Not exactly what we've been doing, but why. He said he'd come by and take you to a hotel so you can sleep. You've been down here for hours. He called Rachel to tell her the two of you are having a nice night of it and that you're not driving home."

"I told her before I came here that I was going to kill Harlan." Emerald said that was smart of him. "I just hope she won't ask me any questions about it. I don't know what I'll tell her if she does."

"You tell her the truth. That he's dead and taken care of." Sean asked if she'd ask more. "She might. You tell her she doesn't want to know. That usually works for me. People are afraid of me, and rightfully so. If she asks you if you killed him, you can truthfully tell her that I did."

Nodding to himself, he turned off the water. A towel appeared in front of him, and he dried himself from top to bottom. The more he thought about what he'd done, the more of it he could justify. Harlan was dead and gone. As far as Sean was concerned, in his heart and head, what he'd done was good. No other child would suffer.

As Chase took him to the hotel, he wondered briefly if Emerald had given him those thoughts and feelings. If she did, then he was fine with that. She was a good person. A wonderful being. He was going to have to thank her for her help.

"I wouldn't if I were you." He looked at Chase as he helped him up to his room. Sean was feeling a little weak, his body worn out. "Don't thank Emerald for this. Whatever you do from now on will be thanks enough for her."

"She won't take it well, I think you're telling me." Chase just laughed. "You might be right. But will you at least thank her for covering for me? For…well, for stopping me too."

"Yes. If you do something for me." He told his brother anything. "The next time you have to kill someone like this, let one of us do it for you—the same as we'd have you do for us. Monsters need to be put down; I can't fault you for that. But going home as if nothing happened isn't going to be easy. If you ever need this done again, I'll come in and do it for you."

"Yes. All right."

Once his brother left, Sean laid on the bed. He was nearly asleep when he reached out to Rachel. He told her that he loved her. *I'm coming home in the morning. I don't think I can face you tonight.*

You'd better. This is something we both needed to be finished. If I could have done it, I would have. He told her it was over. *Good. You sleep well, and I'll see you tomorrow. I love you, Sean Crosby.*

And I love you, my heart.

Sean closed his eyes and let sleep roll over him. He was sore. While he didn't allow his mind to dwell too much on the whys, he did know he'd not be sore like this ever again if he could help it. "I love you too, Jon."

Sleep took him under. Again, just as he was falling into it, he wondered about Emerald. He didn't care. He was ready to sleep now, and that is what he did.

Epilogue

Franklin was both sad and glad that they'd stopped having reunions. Not only had it been difficult for their town to hold all the extra people that came in from all over the world, but also their homes. Hundreds—no, thousands of family members came together to see each other and to eat. He thought for a while there that they'd have to purchase a grocery store just to have it stocked up for the event.

Now they met in groups throughout the year. He thought that was much better. There was more mingling and talking to those he'd not seen in a while. He was glad they didn't have the event yearly. It would have been too much for anyone to handle, he thought. Though no one complained.

Franklin was rocking on the swing when Peter, one of Sean's sons, came to join him. He was the spitting image of his father in all ways but his looks. All the kids the couple had adopted seemed to act a great deal like his son. Even the small mark he'd been given by Queen Killian was there for all to see.

"Well, what do you have to say for yourself, young man?"

Peter grinned at him. So much like his mother in that. "I'm right proud of you and Kiley, Peter. I don't think a person could be prouder of anyone right now."

"Mom is about to bust something, trying hard not to be all mushy with me. I'll have to cut her some slack when I go back home. Who told her to be like that around me today?" Franklin thought it was something she'd thought up herself and told her son that. "Well, I don't care for it. She can hug on me all she wants as far as I'm concerned. We've worked very hard on this, and I couldn't have done it without her pushing me all the time when I was younger."

Franklin reached over and patted Peter's hand, and then hugged him. When they parted, neither of them said anything for a few minutes. Franklin wanted to just bask in the knowledge that one of his people was in the White House and President of the United States.

"Also, I've not told Mom yet, Grandda, but Kiley is going to have a baby." Another hug. Tears this time too. "A Crosby born in the White House. Who would have ever thought it?"

"I did. Perhaps not the Big House, but I knew you were for great things. That momma of yours, she pushed all her kids to be something more than a very wealthy person with magic. When she told me not to buy you a car when you were sixteen, I wanted to do it anyway. But she was right in that. Making you work for it surely did make you appreciate it better. You still drive it, don't you?" Peter laughed and said that Kiley did now. "Now that's a woman after my own heart, that Kiley of yours. She started pushing you into things more than your momma did, I think."

"She said she was glad for the money, but there wasn't any way she was going to be taking it when she was quite capable of working. Not that we didn't enjoy it when we could, but she and I both wanted to work." Same as his momma and daddy. "Grandpa, I was wondering something the other day. It was about my Grandma Rena. Do you think she would have had more children with you, as Brandy did? I love that you and her did. It certainly made for a very large family. But what would have happened should she have not died?"

Franklin rocked for several minutes. One of his daughters came around the side of the house and waved at the two of them. She was fat with a child of her own and as happy as he'd been when her mother had come to him. Franklin thought about his answer even as he told it to Peter.

"We didn't talk about it much. I think she might have wanted more if we'd all been granted the magic we got after she was gone." Peter said he'd not thought of that. "She would have loved all this, all these kids and grandchildren. But even with the magic, I don't think she would have wanted more. Rena wasn't happy being a vampire. I never knew that until later, after I was the sole parent for your uncles and father. Even as a child, her mother told me that Rena would stay out too late in the morning and try to go out too soon in the night. I don't think she loved being a creature of the night as much as most vampires do."

"Do you think she would have ended her life anyway? Even without the humans taking her?" Franklin said yes and let it go at that. "I'm sorry, Grandda. I didn't mean to upset you."

"It's all right, Peter. There are times when I wonder myself if she let herself get caught." He'd never voiced that to anyone before. This thing had been praying on his mind for centuries. "Now, let's not talk about sad things. When is it you're going to be going to the Big House? I know it'll be soon."

"January." Franklin said he thought he knew that in some part of his mind. "Kiley and I are going to move to a hotel in DC so we can be close to things. Sort of get used to the way things are there. Not that we've not worked there for some time now, but it's all different with her being the president."

Yes, sir. She was going to make a fine president too, Franklin thought. As the two of them talked back and forth, something kept nagging at him to ask the younger man. It wasn't important, but it was something he wanted to ask. Looking at the boy who had come to the family late one night, starved and battered, he asked him what he knew of the men who had hurt him.

"Nothing. Not anything at all. Aunt Emerald, she told me it was better for me if I just let it be. I didn't think she was right, but since I've spoken to her recently, she told me that they were no more, and they can't hurt anyone else. I think that was what was giving me nightmares for so long. Thinking that there were other children out there that were being hurt by them." Peter looked beyond where they were seated, to the line of trees that hid Sean's home from this one. "If I'd not been hurt by them, I would never have met Kiley. I knew who she was to me even as a kid of fourteen. Her waiting for me to grow up and to be with her is another thing I wouldn't have had if they'd not taken me. She never aged anymore after we met, and that made things perfect for the two of us. Mom and Aunt Jewel, they told me that when something happens in your life, you can either let it take you under or you learn to live with it. I let it take me for a long time. Then one day, this older vampire came to see me and knocked me around a bit, and I realized I had a great deal to live for. I'll never be able to thank you enough for that, Grandda."

"You were being a little shit to everyone, and I just didn't like it." They both laughed. "I hated that, to have to talk to you that way, but you needed someone to step in. Your daddy would have done it too if he wasn't so busy all the time trying to make your momma stop crying. You hurt her something terrible."

"I did. And I tell her how sorry I am about my beginnings as a Crosby every time I speak to her." Franklin told him he'd better never forget what they'd done for him. "Never. So long as I live, I will never forget anything that everyone in this family has done for me and the rest of this family."

Franklin stayed where he was after Peter was called away. It was like this every time some of the children, grown up adults now, came around. He'd sit out here on the swing and wait for some of them to come and see him. It was wonderful to him that they still included him in their lives.

Cody joined him some time later, telling him about the Crosby Nursery he'd opened up recently in California. They had them all over the country now. Elliot and Cody still ran the one here in town and had the best flowers and trees anyone had ever seen.

Then he had a visit from Jon, Sean's son. My goodness,

he was a tall young man. Handsome too. Jon had written a book about his life when he'd been just a kid, and it had hit the bestseller list. For about three months, it was in the first position on that list, too.

The two of them talked about this and that, and then Jon told him he was writing again, his tenth novel. It was also about dealing with being abused and hurt by those that were supposed to love you. Franklin was very proud of the kid. Three of his books had been made into movies. He was a wonder, Jon was.

When Emerald sat down on the floor in front of him, Franklin waited for her to speak first. It was the way the two of them had been doing this for years upon years.

"There are two things I think you should be made aware of." He nodded and didn't ask. She'd tell him or not. While he loved this woman to pieces, she still scared him a bit. She knew it too. "Were you aware that there are squatters on your land? The scrub land that is just between our house and yours?"

"I did. They're not squatters so much as people trying to ilk out a living by cleaning up the deadfall and the brush thereabouts. I hired them to do it when I found them there about starved a few weeks ago. Did you run them off?" She just glared at him. Franklin couldn't help it; he laughed at her. "Emerald, I don't know if you're aware of this or not, but I don't have to run everything I do by you. I'm a grown man, in the event you might have missed that."

"You're an old poop if you want to know the truth of it. All right. I'll call the pack off — for now. They're doing a good job of it. I've never thought of having that area cleared out." He said he'd not either until he had to find them something to get paid for. "Proud, are they?"

"Yes. Did you know there are three homes in town that are looking for help with some chores? I've hired the oldest boy they have there to do some of the fixing ups for them." She told him she'd noticed that. "Good. I'm glad I could make you think I wasn't feeble."

"You're in a shitty mood. Why is that?" He said he didn't know, just feeling sort of nasty today. "Do you want me to tell you the rest of what I know, or let you stew in your old pile of shit for a little while longer? You should realize you're scaring the children with that frown on your face."

"Tell me what it is you think I need to know." She didn't say anything, and he looked at her. "I am having a shitty day today. I don't know how much you know about the comings and goings of everyone, but today isn't a good day for me. I just want to wallow in my pile of shit a little bit longer."

"No. I don't think you should." He asked her why her opinion should mean two shits to him. "Because I love you, you cantankerous fuck head, and I hate seeing you this way. What's up? Tell me, or I'll go looking for it."

"They don't need me anymore." She asked him what the fuck he was talking about. "Always one for a good comeback, aren't you? Things just go on around them, and here I sit with a nasty dragon queen while she insults me for every little thing."

"Who the hell shit in your oatmeal today?" This time Franklin glared at her. "You are aware that you have about fifty or so family members here that are staying away from you because you're giving off enough bad vibes to make them think you don't want them around. Do you have any idea how many times one of us has had to tell them you're not angry, just an old bastard that wants everyone to go away?"

"You did not tell them that." She smiled at him. "Well, it does sound like something you'd say to people. I'm just in a mood, Emerald. I don't know why or what the mood is about, but mostly it's that they're all grown up and have families of their own. I do too, but like the others, they're making their own way in this world."

"And you don't think you have anything to contribute to them? That's the stupidest thing I think you've ever said, Franklin. You have said some really stupid things too." He told her to go away. "No, not until I get you in a place that you'll listen to me about the second thing."

"You told me. Everyone is afraid to come over here and talk to me." She said there was more. "Well? Spit it out, why don't you? I don't have all day, you know."

"Yes, you do. You have many lifetimes left." She looked behind her, and he did too. Chase was there, holding his youngest grandchild. "Do you know what? I think you're not lonely so much as bored. You don't have anything to occupy your mind, so you're taking it out on everyone else."

"I am bored, damn it. All you people have shit that is getting done. I know I could join in on any one of them if I wanted, but I want something of my own. Something I can be proud of." She asked him if he'd looked around lately. "Yes, why do you think I'm bored? Everyone is out there working, and I'm not."

"So, get a fucking job, moron." He hated it when she called him that. "Besides, I wasn't asking you about what they're doing to make themselves a place in this world, but showing you that without you, without your love and support every single day, none of us would be here. Not one soul would be having children. There would be no faerie queen. No faeries either. The magic that each of us uses every day wouldn't be around for us. There is no telling what your sons would have been like without you there for them. You, you shithead, are the only reason any of us are as happy as we are now. Well, until you started showing your ass and being an old fart."

"I'm entitled to be whatever I want." He realized how childish that sounded as soon as it left his mouth. "Look. You know as well as I do that the fates would have made sure that my boys would have found their mates. It's the way it's written. You know that as well as I do."

"What I know is that Jason would be dead." Franklin asked her what she was talking about. "You know just what I mean. Had you not been there after Jewel knocked him out, Jason would have continued pounding his rules into her, and Jewel would have killed him. Nothing would have saved him either. None of you had immortality as yet. Then there is Brandy and those baby vamps that were set on killing her. They would have too. She would never have made it as a vampire with them. You saved her life, as you had your sons', on a lot of things."

He sat there thinking about all the things she was talking about and more. The other times he'd stepped in to help out his sons. As much as Franklin didn't want to believe her, he knew that on some level, she was right. Emerald told him she was always right.

"Don't read my mind." She told him it was right there on his face. She didn't need to read it to see what he was thinking. "Emerald, would they have done all right without me around? I know you can tell me. Had I been able to join Rena after she was killed, would my sons have fared as well as they have?"

"No. They'd all be dead for a very long time too. I'm not just saying that so I can shake you out of this mood you're determined to be in. But the truth of the matter is, without your guiding hand, Franklin, I'd be dead as well." He asked her how. "With the queen and her magic gone, I would never have been able to survive. The dragons would all be gone from this world because there were no faeries to share what they have with them. I want you to think about what this world would be like if you'd not gathered your boys up and saved the queen of faeries. There would be no sons of Crosby. Nothing to mark what they did in this world. The children we've all had a part in saving, they'd be gone. People would still be starved and out of work. Nothing, not one single thing in this world around us, would ever have or will go on without you. You had the biggest job of all, and you didn't back down from it. You made us what all of us are. Despite you sitting here and feeling sorry for yourself."

She was right. He again didn't want to tell her that, but she was correct. He thought about the argument he'd had with his beloved that morning. It was the reason he'd been sitting out here in the cold while she was out with the others.

"I pissed off Brandy. Not just today like I was thinking, but for a while now. I think she's thinking I don't love her. That I wish I'd joined Rena. I never thought of that, I swear it." Emerald said it didn't matter if he had or not. It was her heart that was broken. "Yes, I guess you're right. Once again. I hate feeling sorry for myself, and I think I was taking that out on her. She's been good for me, you know. I have ten children now. Six of the best sons a man could ask for, and four of the most beautiful daughters that ever touched this old man's heart."

Emerald stood up, and he did as well. When she wrapped her arms around him, Franklin started crying. She'd beaten his mood out of him, and he loved her for it. While she still held him, she whispered in his ear.

"Franklin, you need to go into the house and find Brandy. She's hurting badly right now." Franklin said it was all his fault. "Yes. I'm not going to bullshit you about it either. Go and tell her you're sorry, then I want you to go and see the rest of the family before they have you committed. They're about to rebel at having this shindig at your home from now on."

Thanking her again, he entered his home. It was a home too. Brandy had made it that way. Going to the kitchen, knowing that was where she'd be, he found her kneading bread, her favorite way of letting go of her stress.

"I love you, Brandy. And I'm sorry." Hugging her felt wonderful, and his heart broke when she started crying. "I'm so very sorry. I'll be better. I promise you."

"You'd better." She pulled away from him. "Which one had a talk with you? I'm thinking Jewel. No, not her. Emerald. She'd be just the right person to get you in here."

Kissing her, he laughed, telling her over and over again how much he loved her. Walking hand in hand with her after she finished up the bread, he went to find some babies to hold. His babies, all of them. He was more glad right now than he'd ever been that Emerald had come into their lives.

~*~

Sean made his way home at about midnight. Rachel had left earlier, saying that she needed to get some things finished up before the dinner tomorrow night. Even as he walked into the house, he could hear her talking to herself, a habit she'd picked up from his dad.

"Of course you'll be the one that comes in late. Aren't you always late?" She paused in berating herself. "No. Not always. Just since you've been old."

Laughter, he heard, was her answer to being old. Going into the living room where she was sitting on the floor with papers in front of her, he asked her what she was doing. Her look to him made him think he should have known why she was home.

"I'm grading papers, as I told you I was going to do when I left you." She folded her arms over her breasts. "Do you have any idea how many times I've been grading papers while you're out having fun? Too many to count."

"Then why are you teaching?" He sat down on the couch, the only area that didn't have stacks of paper. "If I remember correctly, you told me you were retiring if Peter and Kiley made it to the White House. Well? Do you want to retire?"

"Yes. Badly." He asked her to come sit on his lap. "I can't leave without grading these papers, Sean. I've been putting it off for too long as it is. They're needing their grades on these."

"I'll help you." He picked up the stack next to him and closed his eyes. Telling the paperwork to make corrections on the stack, he set them aside then looked at Rachel. "Now, what did I do?"

"You could do that all this time?" He nodded, wondering why she sounded so pissed off. "And you didn't think to share it with me? Damn it, I could have had this shit done weeks ago if you'd have told me about that."

"I'm sure you can do it as well." She picked up the stack and did the same thing he had done. When she smiled, he knew it had worked. "I think you can even have the grades put into that book of yours. I mean, even if you can't, this has to save you a ton of time. Right?"

"Yes." She picked up her grade book and laid it on top of her stack of graded papers. After telling it to put the grades into the book, she picked it up and squealed when she saw it had worked. "I should have known this before. Christ, when I think of how many times I got up from the bed to come down here and work. I could have slept better."

"I'm sorry. I don't know why I didn't show you that." He leaned back as she started picking up the six more stacks of paperwork surrounding her. When she was finished, she did finally sit on his lap. "Peter is happy. I saw him earlier tonight talking to Dad. I think whatever they said to each other, it helped Dad. Of course, it could have been Emerald too. I bet she had a few choice words to give him. He was in a much better mood after that."

"I'm glad. I've been worried about him for the last couple of weeks. It's like he was a shell of his former self." Sean held her in his arms as they talked about his dad. "The rest of our family is going to be in DC for the swearing in service for Kiley. I'm so excited to see them again."

"I am as well. Jason was all silly about his newest grandchild. I think it's the first time he's been this over the moon about one of his grandchildren." She asked if it was his first granddaughter. "Yes. He was telling the two-week-old that she was going to have whatever she wanted from him. Of course, he did say that to his grandsons too. I know how he feels about a granddaughter, however. They sort of do make you feel different than having a grandson. But I love them all the same."

He and Rachel had fourteen children and too many grandchildren to count. Some were adopted; some of them were of their blood. Rarely did he ever think of any of them in any way but of his body because they owned his heart. All of them did. Remembering something, he asked her how Becky was doing.

When Rachel tensed up, he knew something had happened. Asking her about it, she told him that Becky and Jon had called her earlier tonight. That speaking to Jon had cleared up a great deal for her.

"Becky is going away in about a month. She said she feels like she can do more work as a doctor in the poorer areas of the world. I don't want her to go. I love having her so close to us all the time. But Jon told me it was more than just that, her going to help out. That she was feeling pulled in that direction. That something or someone needed her." Rachel looked at him. "Do you think it's the pull of a mate?"

"I don't know. I hope so. She's been a little lonely, I think since Jon found his mate." Rachel agreed with him. "Also, and this just could be me hoping, she might well come home feeling like her old self again."

After her mother, Sandy, had been sent to prison for the crimes against her and Jon, Becky had been fine with her life. Or so they had all assumed. Then about six months after Sandy had been out of their lives, she had called to speak to her children. That hadn't gone over well with any of them. But Becky and Jon made the trip with them, and they stayed with them while she was brought into the room to talk to them.

He would never forget the look on everyone's faces when Sandy was uncuffed to sit in front of the windowed area that separated her from them. Pulling out a shiv or whatever it was she'd brought out with her, Sandy slit her own throat. She never said a word to anyone as she lay there dying. But her manic laughter made him cringe every time he thought about it.

Becky had taken it differently than Jon had. In retrospect, he'd thought Jon was the one that had been having the issues with what his mother had done when all along it had been Becky trying to deal with the trauma and the horrific things that had been done to her. Primarily by her mother.

A year after Sandy's death, Becky went into a spiral of anger and being out of control. She attempted suicide several times. Her grades took a nosedive. No one could reach her, not even Jon. It had taken putting her in an institution for a couple of months to get her to the point where she was able to cope with life again. It wasn't the rape that Sean had taken away from her that caused it, but everything else in her young life. Too much horror had taken the child under.

"I want to believe she's finally coming to terms with her life. For a while there, I was worried she'd figure out a way to end her life. I know we're all immortal, but Becky knew that Emerald or Chase could end her life. I think she had been going to the two of them for days before it became clear to the rest of us that she was having issues." Sean nodded. It had broken his heart to see Becky like that. "The best we can hope for is that she is really on a path to recovery. And that she keeps coming to us when things begin to change for her again."

The sun was coming up when they made their way to bed. There were others in the house—a few relatives had stayed with them, as well as some of their own children. But they were all quiet now. When they'd arrived a couple of days ago, he thought for sure that he was going to need to move out to the barn. It was too much after having no one in the house for so long.

"Tomorrow, after the dinner, I'd like for us to have a movie night with the kids." He asked her if she realized they had like sixty people in the house. "I know. But it will be fun. I want to just share something with them again. You think they'll be up for it?"

"If you ask them, yes. Besides, they'll do just about

anything for you, my dear. You're their mother, after all." She snorted at him. "Such a ladylike response."

"I think I might have not given you ladylike responses since we met." He laughed and told her she'd been a pistol. "Anyway, I've been thinking of things like that all day. Having a movie night with the kids. Perhaps pulling out the things I've been saving for them to take home with them. I have so many of their projects that we're going to run out of room when the grandchildren start making things for us."

"We'll build another house for them." She thought he was joking, but it had been a thought of his for the last several months. Not to have a new house to hang the things that the children had given them or made for them, but to have more of their family around. Not to mention, if they were to have a house around, perhaps they'd stay longer. "Do you suppose it would be better if we were to build a hotel so that anyone and everyone that wanted to come here to visit would have their own space? I know they don't mind staying here, but I bet they'd feel better, especially when they think the children are too much for us with having their own space. I don't have any idea why they'd think that when we look as young and feel as young as they do. They can leave their kids here, and they can go to the hotel for all I care."

Rachel smacked him and laughed. Lying down next to her, he felt like he was lucky, in so many ways, as a man. He had the best wife, children, and family. Sean loved them so much that words to convey it were shallow in expressing his true feelings. Closing his eyes, he held onto Rachel. Tomorrow would be a good day. A better day, because he had the love of his life with him.

Before You Go...

HELP AN AUTHOR

write a review

THANK YOU!

Share your voice and help guide other readers to these wonderful books. Even if it's only a line or two, your reviews help readers discover the author's books so they can continue creating stories that you'll love. Log in to your favorite retailer and leave a review. Thank you.

Kathi Barton, a winner of the Pinnacle Book Achievement award as well as a best-selling author on Amazon and All Romance books, lives in Nashport, Ohio, with her husband, Paul. When not creating new worlds and romance, Kathi and her husband enjoy camping and going to auctions. She can also be seen at county fairs with her husband, who is an artist and potter.

Her muse, a cross between Jimmy Stewart and Hugh Jackman, brings her stories to life for her readers in a way that has them coming back time and again for more. Her favorite genre is paranormal romance, with a great deal of spice. You can visit Kathi on line and drop her an email if you'd like. She loves hearing from her fans. aaronskiss@gmail.com.

Follow Kathi on her blog: http://kathisbartonauthor. blogspot.com/